HER CHRISTMAS PREGNANCY SURPRISE

HER CHRISTMAS PREGNANCY SURPRISE

JENNIFER FAYE

MILLS & BOON

PROLOGUE

October...
Ross Tower, New York City

WAS THIS REALLY HAPPENING?

An invitation to one of the most exclusive parties in New York City. It didn't get much better than this.

Okay, it wasn't quite an invitation. Still, she was here among the crème de la crème of New York society—actresses, models, politicians, and the list went on. How she got here shouldn't matter, right?

And, okay, she just happened to be one of the waitstaff. Not an actual guest. But still, this wasn't just any party. This was Simon Ross's party at the top of the tower. She stifled a squeal of delight as she considered pinching herself just to make sure this was real.

Pepper M. Kane resisted the urge, but barely. After all, she had landed—correction, her bakery had landed—this prime opportunity, and she wasn't going to do anything to ruin it or her reputation. If she could make a good impression here, the connections and possibilities were endless.

By the end of the party, she'd handed out countless business cards. Her cheeks were sore from smiling so much. And her feet ached from the heels she'd decided to wear instead of her usual flats. She couldn't wait to get home, curl up on the couch and put on an old black-and-white movie from her ever-growing collection.

There were still a few lingering guests, not to mention the host—the very sexy host. Her gaze moved across the spacious conference hall. There stood the man himself. More than six feet of tall dark sexy goodness.

She clearly remembered their first meeting this past summer. It had been very early one morning when Simon had strolled into the Polka Dotted Bakery. It had been just like any other day when her life started to change. There had been no lightning strikes and no earthquakes, but his entrance into her life had caused ripples through her heart.

At the time, she'd thought he was just another customer. Well, not just any customer—he'd been the only customer at that early hour. Even the sun hadn't risen yet.

Pepper remembered quite clearly that particular morning. She'd been working the front counter when he'd stepped up to the glass display case to peruse the baked goods, from croissants to donuts to cookies and everything else in between. He'd chatted with her about her selection of donuts. And then he'd ordered two coffees, plus two cherry turnovers. After he paid for them, he'd handed her the second coffee and the extra turnover. No one had ever done something like that for her before. She was truly touched.

He had a billion-dollar smile that could melt the frosting right off Pepper's triple-chocolate cupcakes. And he had these dreamy espresso brown eyes that she could stare into the entire day. With his short-styled hair and designer suit, he could easily grace the cover of any magazine or romance book.

The longer she talked to him, the more she'd noticed that he had something weighing on his mind. Pain flared in his eyes. It touched her, and though they were strangers, with her staff handling things in the kitchen, she'd invited him to sit and drink his coffee with her.

He hadn't said much at first, but as one thing led to another, their conversation deepened. And then he'd revealed that he'd just received news that a childhood friend had died. Pepper never thought anything good would come from losing her mother and grandmother, but she was able to draw upon that experience to give some sort of comfort to Simon. It was as though that morning they'd formed a bond—a bond forged in loss and wrapped in hope.

And so for the past five months, Simon had been stopping by the bakery at least once a week early in the morning for two large black coffees and two cherry turnovers. Pepper looked forward to those mornings as they chatted about current events, the bakery or whatever was on their minds. She had made a new friend—a good friend.

And then out of the blue, he'd offered her the opportunity to cater for the Ross Toys expansion party. At first, he'd caught her off guard, as they hadn't exchanged last names. But when she found out he was Simon Ross of Ross Toys she was left speechless. For Pepper, it was a crowning achievement. Ross Toys was one of the biggest businesses in the country.

Today Mr. Ross, as she insisted on calling him

at the party, was the host and she was the baker. Today they were not coffee mates or friends. They each had a job to do—expectations to be met. The announcement of a new chain of stores had been made to the world—Ross Pet Playground. Speeches had been made. Thank-you's had been issued. And predictions were bandied about while Pepper and her staff kept the trays on the buffet table filled.

Pepper had just returned from helping her staff load the empty trays into the delivery van. With both employees and the carts, the van was full. She'd sent her staff back to the bakery to unload and then head home. She'd driven separately, but before leaving, she had to finish cleaning up.

She rushed in the back door and came to an abrupt halt. There stood Simon Ross not more than ten feet from her. He wasn't just another New York City businessman. He had been voted the city's sexiest bachelor, as well as Business Person of the Year, in addition to being CEO and founder of Ross Toys. He was quite a package for some lucky lady.

At the moment, he was deep in conversation with another man in a similar dark suit and tie. Before she could discreetly make it past the men, Simon's gaze met hers. It was only for the briefest of moments, but it was long enough for her heart to start racing. Heat rushed to her face. What was wrong with her? Why couldn't she treat him like any other client?

A mocking voice inside her head said it was because he wasn't like any other client. He'd started off as her friend. And then there was the part about him being smoking hot. She didn't know a man could look that good in a suit.

She moved to the buffet tables, finding them still covered with fine white table linens and a cake platter. She lifted the end of a long white linen—

"Would you like a hand?"

She didn't have to turn around to know that deep, smooth voice belonged to none other than Simon. Her stomach shivered with nerves. She glanced over her shoulder as he moved next to her. "Thanks. But I've got this. Don't you have to tell your guests good-night?"

He frowned.

"I'm sorry." That hadn't come out like she'd intended. "I didn't mean to sound dismissive. I just don't want to take you away from your guests."

"They've all gone now." A smile returned to his very handsome face, making her heart beat faster. "So tell me, what needs to be done?"

Pepper could fold the cloth herself. She'd done it countless times in the past, but she'd been hoping all evening to have a little of his time.

"You could help me fold the tablecloth."

He moved to the other end of the table and lifted the corners of the cloth. They approached each other. Her gaze caught and held his. Her pulse raced and her knees felt as though they'd turned to gelatin. With concerted effort, she kept putting one foot in front of the other. All the while, she wondered if he could hear the pounding of her heart.

And when they brought the material together, their fingers brushed. A jolt of awareness had her gaze dipping to his mouth—his very kissable mouth. The tip of her tongue moistened her lips.

For the longest second of her life, neither of them pulled away. In fact, it was as if time had slowed down. A rush of energy pulsated through her body.

This was ridiculous. It wasn't like this wealthy, extremely handsome, very eligible CEO would be interested in her. She was just a baker with a polka-dotted apron and her hair pulled up. And she was his friend. Nothing more. Just someone to occasionally start the day with over a cup of hot coffee—even if those were the days she most looked forward to.

She moved her hands to lift the fold. "Mr. Ross, I think you had a very successful event."

He arched a brow. "Since when do you call me anything but Simon?"

She glanced around to make sure no one overheard them. "It's different here. Someone might overhear."

"And that would be a problem?"

He was right. She was getting too worked up about protocol and appearances. Still, she couldn't resist glancing around again just to make sure no one was watching or listening to them. Satisfied they had some privacy, she began to relax.

"Congratulations on the new store chain." She took the tablecloth from him, in order to make the final folds. "Your guests all seemed excited about the plan."

"Thanks. It won't be long now. The first store opens just before Christmas."

"Can I ask you a question?"

He shrugged. "Sure."

"If you like animals enough to start up a chain of pet stores, why don't you own one?"

* * *

Simon didn't want to think about the past and how he'd wanted a puppy so badly. Yet the door to the past had been cracked open and now the memories slithered through, filling his mind.

He remembered the little black puppy he'd fallen in love with. The neighbor's dog had given birth. And his best friend, Clay, had offered him a puppy. He'd snuck it home, not wanting anyone to know—if they didn't know, they couldn't ruin this for him.

Except two days later, his father found out and there'd been a high price to pay. Simon absently rubbed his right arm. He slammed the door on the memories. He wasn't going to open up about his horrific past, not even for the amazing woman standing next to him.

"It's not a chain of pet stores. It's a toy store for pets."

"There's a difference?"

He nodded. "We won't be selling food and basics. We'll tailor our supplies to keeping the consumers' four-footed friends entertained." A frown came over his face. "As for me not owning a pet, it's the way I like it."

"Sorry. I didn't mean to overstep."

He cleared his throat. "I think we both had

a successful evening. Are all of your business cards gone?"

"Almost." She pulled a dozen or so out of her pocket.

"I predict you're going to be very busy in the near future."

"I hope so."

"Trust me. I see a brilliant future for you." He smiled at her.

Her stomach dipped. No one had a right to have such a sexy smile. What were they talking about? It took her a second, but then she got her mind back on track.

Her gaze met his and held, much, much longer than was necessary. Her heart started to beat faster. "I... I want to thank you for hiring me—for hiring the bakery—my bakery."

Oh, why am I tripping all over my words? It's not like this is a date or anything.

He smiled. "There's no need to thank me. I wanted the best. And you are the best."

Pepper felt as though her feet had just left the floor. He thought she was the best? Her lips pulled up into a big, broad smile as her heart continued its erratic *tap-tap-tap-tap*. It was like it was beating some Morse code signal or something.

"Yes, there is. It means a lot that you think enough of my baked goods to want me to serve a party."

He continued to stare deeply into her eyes. "Of course, I think your food is amazing. But I didn't hire you."

"You didn't?" She studied him, not sure what to think.

He shook his head again. "I have staff that take care of things like that."

"Of course you do," she mumbled under her breath. The blaze of heat singed her cheeks as she glanced away. What made her think he would be bothered hiring a caterer?

"Not that I wouldn't have hired you." His gaze met hers yet again. "It appears I'm not the only one to think you have the best bakery in the city."

Once again the heat flamed in her cheeks. She glanced up. "Thank you. I should be going." When he didn't make any move to leave, she said, "I'm sure you have other plans."

She wanted to ask if he had a girlfriend, but it was absolutely none of her business. And she didn't want him thinking she was hitting on him—that would be the end of their easy friendship. Besides, a friendship was as much as she was willing to offer anyone. The thought of caring for someone—of losing another person in her life—scared her.

"For once, I don't have plans."

And so he lingered while she placed the tablecloth in a box with some other items. "You must always be so busy. I can't even imagine what it would be like to run a company this size. I know that my little bakery keeps me busy from morning until night." She was running out of things to say, but he still didn't make any movement to leave.

"Usually, I spend my evenings in the office."

"So you like to stay on top of everything?"

He nodded. "I do." He started helping her pick up things. "Just like you do by being here for the party."

Heat rushed to her cheeks. He was referring to the fact that she was here in person instead of sending someone from her staff. "The truth is I like to handle these events."

He arched a dark brow. "You like to make connections and expand your business. And your staff can't do that as well as you do. I totally understand. You and I, we aren't so different. If you ever want to discuss your business model or plans, let me know."

Pepper couldn't believe what she was hearing. Simon Ross, *the* Simon Ross, was offering to help her with her business. Like he didn't already have his hands full with a Fortune 500 company that kept rising in people's estimations. If anyone could help her, it would be him. She'd love to hear what he had to say.

"Thank you," she said, carefully placing a stray cake server in the box. "I'd really appreciate it. Right now, I could take all of the help I can get."

"Do you have any plans for tonight?"

"No. I don't." The words slipped past her lips before her mind had a chance to catch up. Some helpful business advice would be just what she needed. But she sensed he had more than business on his mind.

As though he was reading her thoughts, his gaze dipped to her lips. Could this really be happening? The girl voted most likely to run away with the circus because of her strawberry blond hair and her colorful clothes. The girl who had never fitted in until she opened her bakery. Within those walls, she could unwind and be herself.

He picked up her box from the floor. "Are you ready to go? We can grab a late dinner."

She had to make sure this thing arcing between them was real—that it flowed both ways. And it wasn't some sort of misunderstanding. Staring into his eyes, her heart pounding, she asked, "It isn't business you have on your mind, is it?"

He stepped closer to her. His voice lowered to a sexy, hushed tone. "No. Is that a problem?"

He was giving her an out. Knowing they came from totally different worlds, she would be smart to back away. But she was drawn to him unlike any other man in her life.

Simon didn't see her as the awkward girl in school that never could manage to be just one of the crowd. Those days were in the past—or so she wanted to believe.

When concern touched Simon's eyes, she realized the brief memories of her past had her frowning. She turned that frown upside down and sent him one of her brightest smiles. She was no longer the girl kids would point at and whisper about. Now, she was a confident business owner.

With Simon standing so close to her, she had to tilt her chin upward for their gazes to meet. As she stared into his dark eyes, she felt as though she could get lost in them. She couldn't think of anything she'd rather do than spend the evening with him.

"I'd like to go to dinner with you."

His voice lowered even more. "You don't know how long I've wanted to ask you out."

"Really?"

He nodded. "You intrigue me."

A flutter of excitement filled her chest. "So why didn't you ask me?"

He placed the box on the table next to them. "It was never the right time. I was busy with plans for this new venture. And you were busy with the bakery."

It was true. They were busy people, but she would have made time for him, just as she had in the mornings for coffee over the last several months. It was during those mornings that they'd slowly let their guards down—revealing parts of their lives. But how had she missed that he was interested in her?

He reached out to her. His thumb gently caressed her cheek. "You are so beautiful."

She leaned into his touch. His gaze held hers, as though he needed the connection more than oxygen. And then his gaze lowered just a bit. Her racing heart jolted with anticipation. He was going to kiss her.

The breath caught in her lungs. As his head lowered, she gave herself over to the moment. Her eyes fluttered shut. And then she melted into his very capable arms. Her hands landed against his muscular chest and moved slowly up to his shoulders.

The kiss, though gentle at first, picked up its pace. His mouth moving over hers, his tongue probing her mouth and her giving in to the ecstasy.

Crash!

Pepper jumped back. Her heart careened into her throat. She pressed a hand to her sensitive lips. All the while, her gaze moved about the conference room, searching for the source of the noise. And then she spotted the box on the floor. They must have bumped into it while they'd been kissing.

She scanned the room again. There had been no one else around. Their kiss was still their secret. She liked the thought of sharing a moment of passion with Simon—something only the two of them knew about.

Her gaze returned to the upturned carton. "Oh, what a mess."

"Don't worry. I'll help clean it up."

Together they knelt down, Pepper righting the

box and the few things that remained inside it. Simon handed her the scattered contents. In no time, the mess was cleaned up.

When they'd both straightened, Simon leaned in and pressed a kiss to her lips. It was short, but it left no doubt in her mind that there was chemistry between them—as in the sizzling, smoking, combustible kind.

She swallowed hard as her heart pounded in her chest. All the while, her gaze followed him as he shifted. She should say something. Yes, she should not let on that his touch had rocked her to her very core.

Summoning her wits, she smiled at him. She just couldn't let him see how much he got to her. "What was that for?"

He smiled at her. It was one of those lazy smiles that showed just a bit of his straight, white teeth. Her stomach dipped. No man had a right to be that handsome.

When he spoke, his voice held a rich timbre. "I wanted something to tide me over until dessert."

He was back to flirting with her and she liked it—she liked him. And the way he looked at her, it was like he was making love to her with his eyes. No longer the social misfit, she'd blossomed into Cinderella.

Her gaze strayed across the sharp contours of Simon's face, down to his broad shoulders and muscled chest. Oh, yes, he was definitely her Prince Charming.

CHAPTER ONE

Seven weeks later...

The Polka Dotted Bakery

THERE'S ONE THING about fairy tales...

They don't always have a happily-ever-after.

Not even a happy-for-now.

Pepper glanced out the decorated storefront window and didn't see any paparazzi. She took an easy breath. It was the first time in weeks. Seven whole weeks plus one day of being hounded for photos and comments.

And she was tired. Tired of it all.

But at last, there was peace.

In the end, she'd done nothing wrong. Nothing, except for letting her defenses down with a man that she'd thought— Well, it didn't matter what she thought because she'd been wrong about him, about the evening together, about them. And now, the paparazzi wanted a comment.

She'd been counting off the days since their

night of passion turned into a morning of regrets. It had been fifty days since she'd found herself in the arms of Simon Ross. Forty-nine evenings since she'd spent the most glorious night with him. And seven long weeks since her life had felt like her own.

And a lifetime since she'd last seen him.

Not that she missed Simon…at all. Not a bit.

The very next morning after her fairy tale had begun, her life had spun into some sort of soap opera. One photographer had spotted her leaving Simon's building in the wee hours of the morning. How he'd known she'd come from Simon's place, out of all the condos in the high-rise, was beyond her. Perhaps it was the doorman, or maybe it'd been a nosy neighbor anxious for a quick payoff, or possibly someone had spotted them kissing after Simon's big announcement.

Then Simon had phoned. The first words out of his mouth had been an apology.

Her heart sank down to the tips of her cotton-candy-pink painted toes. It was obvious he regretted their night together, and everything that she'd thought was happening between them had been nothing more than a figment of her imagination. But then he'd sent her a link to a website with a picture of them kissing after the party, and it became clear what he was apologizing for.

Billionaire Bachelor Interviewing New Love Interest!

The headline was outrageous. How had their brief relationship been leaked to the press?

It was then that she knew she had to end things before he did. She told him that they'd just gotten caught up in the moment and it should end right here and now. He hadn't said a word. He obviously agreed. That was it. No discussion. No nothing. The night before, they'd made love, and the next morning, it was over.

Until that moment, she'd never appreciated her freedom to move about the city basically anonymously. For the most part, no one knew her and didn't pay attention to what she did. From that day forward, it was like everything she did had to be analyzed for the world to read and to figure out what, if anything, it had to do with Simon.

A single photographer had quickly turned into a gaggle of them. Keeping them out of the bakery had become a full-time job for her staff. With her apartment above the bakery, there was no getting away from them.

One morning, she'd glanced out her apartment window to find a photographer hanging from the tree. Seriously. He'd just been hanging there like he was part monkey, with a camera in hand. She'd closed her mini blinds and then drawn her curtains. She'd never felt more invaded in her entire life.

But then they'd started dissecting her life, from her mother's death to her life with her grandmother. She'd felt naked and exposed for the whole world to see. She didn't know how Simon lived in the spotlight. And then they'd sought out people who had known her in school. Every insecurity she'd ever had in her youth came rolling back.

Little did the paparazzi know that it'd been nothing more than a brief fling with Simon. She thought of telling the photographers that they were wasting their time, but her wounded pride and the prick to her heart kept the words locked deep inside her.

From One Night to Wedding Bells!

Honestly, who came up with these outrageous and totally false headlines?

Her friends commiserated with her. And told

her to look on the bright side—business at the bakery had never been better. They were right. She was doing a booming business.

And then the next headline came quite unexpectedly.

Billionaire Bachelor Moves On...

One minute the paparazzi had them picking out wedding venues, with a photo of two people who were quite obviously not them, and the next they had him moving on. Although this time the photo was most certainly Simon. He'd been spotted the following week with his arm around a leggy blonde as they attended a Broadway show opening. As Pepper stared at the photo, she resisted admitting to the sharp piercing pain.

So much for their special evening meaning anything to him. Her back teeth clenched together. Lucky for him, he hadn't been back for his weekly order. He might have ended up wearing his coffee.

And the part of her that missed his bright smile and his flirty ways that made her feel like the most beautiful woman in the world? Well, she shushed it right up. He wasn't worth missing.

Simon Ross lived up to his reputation as the un-catchable bachelor.

It didn't help that she hadn't felt great for the past few days. She had a slight headache and she blamed that for her queasy stomach. It wasn't enough to stop her though. Whatever it was, it would pass.

It was no wonder she didn't feel good, aside from the mess with Simon. She had competition. A new bakery had just moved in on the next block. And her business took an immediate hit. Customers strayed to the new place, eager to see what they had to offer.

To that extent, she supposed her friends were right and the coverage about her and Simon wasn't all bad. People had visited the bakery to meet her, but she made sure to stay busy in the back. Still, while they were there, they bought her products. They bought a lot of products. If things had ended better with Simon, she might be inclined to thank him. But as it was, she didn't think she'd ever speak to him again.

The new bakery was pulling out all the stops with big ads, radio spots and every other promotion they could think of. The bakery was part of a national chain that could afford to under-cut their prices to drive the competition out of business. Then once the competitors were out of business, they'd jack up their prices. The nerve of some people.

But Pepper refused to let them drive her out of business—not without a big fight. She'd sunk everything she had into making this bakery a success. It was a dream of hers—a dream that she refused to let die, even if it meant doing things that she wouldn't otherwise have done, like working round the clock if she had to. The chain couldn't keep up their deep discounts forever. At least, she hoped not.

In the meantime, she was taking every Christmas party she could cram onto her calendar. It was exhausting, but her grandmother had always told her that nothing worth having came easily. This bakery definitely wasn't going to be easy.

She worked from the time she woke up, which was hours before the sun decided to rise, until she fell into bed early in the evening utterly exhausted, sometimes still in her work clothes. And so far, it was working. She was keeping her existing clients and gaining new ones. Things at last were looking up. Her clients recognized true quality and not frozen mass product.

Now that Christmastime was here, it was time to sparkle. Pepper loved Christmas above all other holidays. And that was saying something because they all had a special place in her heart. But she not only loved Christmas, she really *loved* it. It was magical and it brought out the best in people. People were a little nicer to others, holding doors, sharing a smile or a nod. If it was possible, she'd have Christmas all year round.

It was almost time to open up for the day. She loved this early morning hour. In her mind, each day was a new beginning with new possibilities. And she had a feeling something big was going to happen. Maybe they'd be hired for the wedding of the year. Or perhaps she'd meet a big client at the holiday party she was catering that evening. A smile pulled at her lips as anticipation put some pep in her step.

She moved to the stereo system and turned it on. Over the speakers came the deep timbre of Michael Bublé's voice as he sang "It's beginning to look a lot like Christmas." She glanced out the window as the flurries swirled through the air. This really was her favorite time of the year.

Yesterday had been Sunday, the only day of the week the shop was closed. She'd taken advantage of the downtime to get out the holiday decorations. It took all day to exchange the

Thanksgiving fanfare for the homey Christmas look, but that was because she'd baked and crafted a lot of the decorations herself.

She paused next to the glass display cases and glanced around at her handiwork. On the brick wall where floating shelves normally displayed an array of antique dishes, she'd replaced them with gingerbread figures, from a giant gingerbread man to a gingerbread train. There were also red ribbons, greenery, pinecones and a poinsettia bloom here and there.

She loved gingerbread. Not only did it taste delicious, but there were so many things to do with it. And so she might have gone a little overboard this year with gingerbread. It was even in the store window.

Looking around at all she'd accomplished, she realized she'd done it all alone. As much as she loved this bakery, she'd give it up to have her family once more. The joy the bakery brought to her life just wasn't the same as having her family by her side, especially during this festive holiday season.

Walking through life alone was not how she'd envisioned her future. And yet that's exactly what she was doing. Because each and every person who meant something to her had been torn from her life.

She'd learned to close her feelings to others little by little, and her grandmother's death had been the last straw. That was it. The protective walls had fully encased her heart. She was done with loving and losing.

Pepper moved to the front door and turned the lock. She smiled as the first rays of sun lightened up the inky sky. Beneath the streetlights, a light coating of snow was detectable. It had fallen last night, coating the grass but leaving the street clear.

"It's going to be a good day. A very good day indeed." If only wishes came true.

"What did you say?" Charlotte asked from behind the counter.

Pepper shook her head. "Nothing important."

Charlotte arched a brow. "Talking to yourself again?" When Pepper shrugged, Charlotte continued, "You keep that up and I'm going to start worrying about you."

Pepper moved behind the counter. Her gaze strayed across the little stuffed dog she'd had since she was a girl. When she was young, they'd lived in an apartment—a small apartment—that didn't allow pets. And she'd wanted a dog in the worst way. Every birthday and Christmas, when anyone asked her what she wanted, she would tell them a puppy.

Her mother felt so bad that she gave Pepper this designer stuffed beagle and a promise that someday when they moved to a bigger place that allowed pets, she would get her a dog. But that day never came.

She'd lost her mother at the tender age of eight, after a car had run a red light and struck her mother as she'd crossed the street. Pepper had gone to live with her grandmother, who was allergic to animals. Bugles McBeagle had come with her.

She sighed as she ran a finger over the dog's plush fur, promising herself that someday she would have her puppy. Just not today.

The business phone rang. Pepper rushed over to answer it. "Hello. This is the Polka Dotted Bakery. How may I help you?"

"Pepper, this is Mike. I'm sorry to do this, but I quit."

"Quit?" Not again.

"I just couldn't say no."

"No? To what? To whom?" She had a sinking feeling she knew who he was talking about, but she had to hear him say it. She needed the confirmation.

"The other bakery. They approached me when I was leaving work yesterday. They offered me a lot more money. And with the baby on the way, we need all of the money I can make. Pepper, if it wasn't for that, I swear, I wouldn't be leaving. Honest."

She liked Mike. He'd been with her since she'd opened the shop. And even though she didn't want to, she understood he had to put the needs of his family before his loyalty to her and the business.

She wished him well and hung up. So now she was short a baker and she had a party to prepare for...alone.

Not wasting any more time, she got to work.

CHAPTER TWO

THIS COULDN'T BE HAPPENING.

How had he let this slip through the cracks?

With the tinted rear windows of the car, no one could make him out. Simon was free to stare at the passing buildings and people hustling along the crowded sidewalk. The Polka Dotted Bakery was a place he'd thought of often in the past several weeks. He tried to tell himself that it was the fragrant and rich coffee that he missed, but it was something more than that. An image of Pepper laughing flashed in his mind. He recalled how her lush lips would part, lifting up at the corners, and her pinkened cheeks would puff up. But more than that, her eyes would twinkle and the green of her eyes reminded him of gemstones.

And then a much more somber memory rushed to the forefront—his last conversation with Pepper. There had been no smiles, no friendliness. She'd dumped him, dismissed him, had no use for him. That was something he was not used to, at all. He was the one who always ended relationships. Not the other way around.

"Pull over here," he said to his driver.

He didn't normally have a driver, but seeing as he was headed for the bakery and parking could be quite limited at this time of the day, he'd decided it would be prudent. He'd considered calling her on the phone, but he didn't feel right about it.

Simon opened the car door and immediately the distinct nip in the air assailed him. The holidays were here and so was the winter season. He tugged at the collar of his black wool overcoat and pulled it close to his neck to keep out the chilling breeze. Not even the midafternoon sun was enough to warm him.

There had been so many times over the past several weeks when he'd wanted to swing by the bakery. He told himself that it was the cherry turnovers that he craved—not staring into the green eyes of the very beautiful baker.

And it didn't help that when he suddenly stopped bringing the mouthwateringly good baked goods to the office it was noticed by his employees. When he got questioned enough about the lack of treats, he started going to the new bakery, though the service wasn't nearly as friendly and the turnovers—well, they were dry and overly sweet. And though his staff didn't say much, the number of leftover pastries at the end of the day said it all.

Though everything in his body wanted to turn around, he kept putting one foot in front of the other. The streets were decorated with garland and on each lamp post was a large wreath with a great big red bow. Shop windows had holiday displays. Some had Santa figurines and others Christmas trees. Everything to put the passerby in the holiday spirit—except for Simon.

However, when he reached the large picture window of the Polka Dotted Bakery, he slowed down. How could he not? The holiday-themed display was literally a work of art—all made out of baked goods.

It was a wintery scene, with a white tree with gingerbread ornaments trimmed with white frosting suspended from it. And beneath the tree was a gingerbread house. Not just four walls and a roof of gumdrops. Someone had gone all out, detailing not a one, not a two, not even a three, but a four-story house decorated with white and pale pink frosting. He didn't have to guess. He knew it was Pepper's work. She was quite talented, making the window shutters out of white frosting, and there was even a chimney.

He drew in a deep breath, straightened his shoulders and opened the glass door of the bakery. When he stepped inside, he found it empty. Not one single customer. Sure, it was a little past three in the afternoon, but from what Pepper had told him, there were usually customers streaming in and out of the bakery all day long.

He stepped further into the shop to find the display cases completely full, as though none of the goods had sold that day. How could this be? Pepper, by far, had the best pastries in the city.

"I'll be right with you." Her voice was light and friendly, just the way he remembered it before things had spun out of control.

He turned to her, bracing for Pepper's onslaught of angry words. She knelt down, placing something in the glass display case. When she straightened—when she saw that it was him and when she heard what he'd come here to tell her—he was certain her tone would change drastically.

And then she straightened with a smile on her face. Her beautiful long auburn hair was pulled back in a twist, pinned to the back of her head. When the lights hit her hair, the deep red highlights shone. Her bangs fell to the side of her face and a few wispy curls fell around the nape of her neck. Was this the real reason he'd come here? To have one more look at her—to drink in her beauty?

As recognition flashed in her eyes, her friendly demeanor vanished in a heartbeat, replaced with a distinct frown. "You." Her green eyes widened with surprise. "What are you doing here?" Then she held up a hand as though stopping him from speaking. "Never mind. I don't want to know. Just leave before someone sees you here."

"Pepper, we need to talk."

She shook her head. "If anyone spots you here, the press with be back. I can't deal with them. Just go."

He knew how bad the paparazzi could be when they were chasing what they thought was a story. "I've taken precautions so no one knows I'm here."

She didn't say anything for a moment. "They'll still find out. They even dug into my past. My past! People I never thought I'd speak to again were giving interviews about me. Do you know how that invasion of privacy felt?"

"I do. And I'm sorry." His whole life had been aired in the papers since his business took off.

It had been hard, but he was somewhat used to it now. "Just hear what I have to say and then I'll go."

She placed her hands on her waist. If looks could vaporize a person, he would be nothing more than mist. Wait. How did she get to be so angry with him? She was the one who had dumped him.

Not that the night would have led anywhere. He didn't do relationships—not even with the very sweet, very tempting Polka Dotted Baker. He wasn't cut out to be someone's boyfriend, much less someone's husband or worse yet, a father.

Still, she glowered at him. He didn't move an inch. If this was a struggle of wills, he would win. He'd come here for a purpose. He thought he was doing a nice thing. Now, he was having second thoughts. Still, he was here. And he wasn't leaving until he'd had his say.

She stared deep into his eyes. "Make it fast."

"Where are all of your customers?" He sensed something was very wrong. "And why does it look like you haven't sold anything?"

"Things have changed. I don't have time to chat. I have work to do." She moved past him, leaving plenty of room between them so their bodies didn't touch.

She stepped up to the front door and flipped the sign to Closed. He couldn't help but notice her craning her neck to gaze up and down the walk, as though checking to see if anyone had spotted him in her shop. As far as he could tell, his ball cap and dark sunglasses had kept his identity under wraps.

"There's something important I need to tell you."

She shook her head. "How about we just go back to pretending we don't know each other? Life was so much easier back then."

He wished he could rewind time. "It's too late for that."

She didn't say anything as she moved past him and kept going toward the back of the bakery. What he didn't understand was her hostility. If he'd dumped her, he'd get it. But she'd been the one to end things. Sure, he'd been getting ready to do it, but she'd beaten him to the punch.

He followed her because he still hadn't told her the reason for his visit. She led him to a small office. The room had vacant white walls, which surprised him after getting to know Pepper's lively personality and her penchant for decorating. A solitary desk in the room was buried beneath a mountain of paperwork. She grabbed a small quilted backpack with a red-and-white pattern, as well as a digital notebook.

When she turned to the door, she practically ran into him. She glanced up as though she'd gotten lost in her thoughts and had forgotten him. His ego was taking hits left and right. He still wasn't sure why she was so steamed with him.

She glanced at her wristwatch. "If you came here to talk about the past, don't. It was a stupid mistake. It won't happen again."

If he'd had any doubt about her sincerity, he had his answer. She wanted nothing to do with him. That was a first for him. She certainly was different than everyone else in his life.

And this was why he'd been drawn to Pepper in the first place. She wasn't a pushover. She wasn't out to see what he could do for her. She was her own woman, who took life on her own terms.

She placed her things on the counter. After washing her hands, she set to work. Pepper continued to move about the kitchen as though he weren't even standing there.

"Why are you so mad at me?" He stood at the

edge of the large kitchen with all its gleaming stainless surfaces. "As I recall, you're the one that dumped me."

Her cheeks filled with color. "I didn't dump you."

She added sugar into a saucepan and placed it on the gas stove. She kept her back to him as she adjusted the temperature. He was in absolutely no mood to be ignored.

"I'm pretty sure you did." His bruised ego could attest to it. "So why all of the hostility?"

She spun around. Her gaze clashed with his. "I'm not hostile."

He arched a disbelieving brow and waited for her to explain herself. He didn't mind taking the heat when he deserved it. But in this case, he didn't do anything wrong. Thoughts of nipping the relationship in the bud didn't count. Pepper might be good at figuring out people, but even she wasn't a mind reader.

She sighed. "You're right. I'm taking my frustrations out on you." She paused as though choosing her words carefully. "I… I'm sorry." Her gaze met his briefly, but she turned away before he could read her thoughts. "Things at the bakery haven't been going well." She took the saucepan and stirred as the sugar began melting. "But you didn't come here to hear about my troubles."

At last, she was beginning to sound like the Pepper he'd gotten to know and trust. "Would you believe I missed your cherry turnovers so much I couldn't stay away?"

She tilted the pan, letting the melted sugar roll across the bottom. She didn't say anything, concentrating on what she was doing.

And that was why what he had to say next was that much harder. He wasn't so sure he wanted to have this conversation while she was distracted, but she wasn't leaving him much choice. She took a spoon with a long round handle and began to drizzle the caramel onto it. All the while, she turned the handle so the caramel would make a corkscrew shape.

He never knew there was so much more to baking than mixing up some delicious-tasting batter and pouring it into a pan. But Pepper was showing him another side of the business and he was enthralled with it. She made it look so easy—like anyone could do it. Even him.

She moved the corkscrew to a piece of waxed paper and then started to make a new one. They were beautiful. They were like little pieces of art.

And the guilt he'd been carrying around with him most of the day mounted.

"Pepper—"

"Just give me one more minute." Her full attention was on her work and he couldn't blame her. What she did here was like magic. If he tried to do the same thing, he'd end up with burnt sugar.

He knew he should hurry. He didn't have that much time to get out of the city and to his country estate, where the big Christmas celebration was taking place. But he didn't move a muscle as he stood there watching Pepper do her thing. Each golden caramel corkscrew was then placed atop a cupcake. They looked too good to eat.

When Pepper had finished with all the cupcakes, she straightened, glanced at him and blinked, as though she'd forgotten that he was still there waiting to talk to her. And then her gaze moved to the clock above his head.

"I have to hurry." Her beautiful face creased with worry lines.

"What happens if you don't finish these?" He knew the stakes were high, but he wondered how high they were.

Pepper shook her head as she boxed up the cupcakes. "That can't happen."

He moved next to her, placing a lid on the full box. "Pepper, stop for just a moment."

She turned to him. "Simon, I'm sorry. I just don't have time to talk. I have a very important party."

"That's the thing."

"What's the thing?"

His gaze met hers. "The party. It's mine."

"Yours?" She shook her head. "I spoke with a woman. Elaine something or other. I have her full name written on the order. And this party is in Connecticut."

He nodded. "Elaine Haskins is my assistant and the party is at my country home."

Pepper's face creased with lines of frustration. She didn't say a word as she digested the information.

"I'm sorry," he said. "This is my fault. Everyone was so impressed with you at the office party that Elaine added you to our catering list. After what happened between us, I forgot to say anything to her. I totally understand you wanting to cancel—"

"Cancel?" Her shoulders straightened and she lifted her chin slightly. "I'm not canceling."

"You're not?" He was so confused.

"We have a contract. I expect you to keep your end of it."

"But why? I mean, why would you want to cater a party for me?"

"Because this is business. It's not personal. I can't believe I have to explain this to you."

And then he thought of the empty bakery and the overabundance of unsold goods. Something had happened to her business, and he wondered if it had anything to do with the paparazzi fuss when they'd caught on to their night together. His jaw tightened. He was so used to it that he hadn't stopped to consider how it might affect Pepper.

"And you don't mind working this party, even though it's for me."

She straightened her shoulders and there was a slight tilt to her chin. "I'm a professional. I can do this job. There won't be any problems."

"I know you are and I didn't mean to imply otherwise." He couldn't shake the thought of the baked goods going to waste in her display cases. "I'll throw in extra if you include everything in your cases."

Her mouth gaped. She quickly regained her composure. "Why would you do that? If you want a cherry turnover that bad, all you have to do is ask."

He would make sure and set those aside for himself. "I have some extra guests," he said, which was the truth, but just part of it. "I want to make sure there's enough for everyone."

"Oh. Okay. I'll get them boxed up."

He glanced around. "Are you the only one here?"

She nodded. "Don't worry. I have a couple employees meeting me at your estate."

"Let me give you a hand." He slipped off his coat.

"You don't have to do that."

"Sure I do. I'm the one who insisted on the extra items. The least I can do is give you a hand boxing them up." He didn't mention that he'd noticed the dark smudges under her eyes. She was working too hard and not getting enough sleep. At least he hoped that's all it was.

They worked together, packing up all the delicious treats. Simon snagged one of the cherry turnovers. He couldn't wait until later. His palate had been in withdrawal for weeks now. He was only so strong.

"Look at the time." There was mild panic in

Pepper's voice. "With the traffic, I'm going to be late."

"Not if you leave now."

"But there's still all of this to load in the van."

"I'll help you."

This time she didn't argue. They moved the baked goods on carts out to the delivery van painted in white with big black polka dots all over it and the logo for the Polka Dotted Bakery painted in bubblegum pink and lime green. He couldn't help but smile. It was unique, just like its owner.

The truck was quite full when they were done and Simon wasn't sure what he was going to do with all the extra food, but he would deal with that problem later.

He climbed out of the back of the van. "You're good to go."

She stood frowning.

"What's the matter?"

"I forgot something." And then her eyes widened. "My backpack. It's on the counter."

When she went to turn and rush back inside, he reached out to her. "You stay here. Close up the van and I'll grab your stuff."

She nodded.

He ran back inside the bakery. The only problem was that there were a lot of counters. His gaze moved around the kitchen in a counter clockwise manner. And then he spotted her red and white backpack as well as the digital tablet next to the stove. He rushed over and grabbed them.

He moved too quickly and the backpack knocked over a tall stack of business cards, as well as some papers. A frustrated groan formed deep in his throat. He rushed to clean up the mess. He guessed that Pepper meant to take the business cards with her to hand out at the party. He took most of them and her backpack. He flipped off the lights, exited the building and, using the keys Pepper had placed in the door earlier, locked it.

She was in the back of the van, doing something with one of the boxes.

"I've got it," he called out.

"Okay. This is all set." She climbed out, closed the door and turned to him. "I just have to set the alarm system."

She rushed back inside. He checked the time. It was most definitely late, and it was his fault for insisting on taking her extra pastries. He owed it to Pepper to make sure she arrived on time. He called his driver to tell him to head to

Connecticut without him. Simon had just hung up when she returned.

"I'm never going to make it on time," she said.

"You will if you take a couple of shortcuts I've learned."

She shook her head. "I'll just get lost. I'm going whatever way my phone app tells me."

"Trust me. I'll show you the way."

"You?" She shook her head. "I don't think so."

"Think of it this way. The longer you stand here arguing with me, the later you'll be."

Her lips pressed together in a firm line. And unhappiness was written all over her face. "Fine. Let's go."

He hadn't imagined the day taking this most unexpected twist. What would they talk about? On second thought, it was probably best to remain quiet. This was going to be a very interesting ride indeed.

CHAPTER THREE

WHAT WAS SHE THINKING?

The last time she'd been alone with this man, her world had come undone. Pepper kept her gaze focused on the busy roadway. But she couldn't ignore Simon's presence. With him next to her, it felt as though the interior of the van had shrunk.

He was so close that she could reach out and touch him—like they'd done after his party to announce the launch of his Pet Playground stores. They'd been hand in hand as Simon drove them back to his place. They'd laughed. They'd talked. The exact opposite of now.

She quietly followed Simon's instructions as she weaved her way through traffic. Even with Simon's input, it still wasn't a quick journey.

And with hustling out the door, she couldn't help but wonder if she'd turned everything off. She hated rushing. It left room for error and she always strived for perfection, though she never reached it. But she'd grabbed everything for the party and she'd set the alarm.

Still, worry niggled at her.

"What's the matter?" Simon asked.

"Did I turn off the lights?"

"You did."

"Did I lock the front door?"

"You did."

"Did I get everything?"

"Pepper, what's the matter?"

She sighed. "I just have the feeling I'm forgetting something."

"I don't think you have to worry. Everything is under control."

She hoped he was right.

Other than some instructions on where to turn, silence fell back over the van. It wasn't a comfortable silence. In place of conversation was a strained void. She should have refused his offer to ride with her. But then she would most definitely be late and that would be very bad, especially if this guest list was anything like his last party.

She couldn't help glancing around in traffic just to make sure the paparazzi weren't following them. Thankfully, they weren't. She glanced over at Simon as he lounged back in his seat, checking messages on his phone.

The silence in the van was deafening. She reached over and turned on the radio. She adjusted the tuner to a station that played nothing but Christmas tunes. Andy Williams's "Sleigh Ride" was playing. At least it was upbeat, unlike her passenger. She turned it up.

She chanced a quick glance at him. The frown on his face had deepened, marring his handsome face with deep lines. What was up with him? Did he regret offering to ride with her?

"Is something bothering you?" The question popped out of her mouth before her brain had a chance to restrain her tongue.

"What?"

At the same time, they reached for the radio. Their fingers touched. A tingle pulsed up her arm. She glanced at him. His gaze met hers, making her heart pound.

She yanked her hand away as she turned her attention back to the road. Simon lowered the volume on the radio. She swallowed hard, gripping the steering wheel with both hands as she tried to put a lid on whatever it was that just happened between them.

"That's better," Simon said. "Now what did you ask?"

She felt really weird asking him now, but she refused to let on how their contact had unnerved her. "Is something bothering you?"

"You mean besides you being angry at me when it was you who dumped me?"

So they were back to this again. "I didn't see you minding so much when you were out with that tall blonde the next night."

"It wasn't the next night." His tone was gruff. "It was two weeks later."

"A day. A week or two. It's the same difference."

"Turn left right up here." He was quiet for a moment. "And it does matter, because it wasn't the same thing."

She made the turn. She shouldn't care, but her curiosity was eating at her. "Why is that?"

"Because that appearance wasn't a date. It was arranged to draw the paparazzi's attention from you."

It wasn't a date? She caught sight of the serious look in his eyes. Should she believe him? After all, they had looked like a real couple in the photo. "But they said you were both on the rebound."

"Turn left in a mile onto Willow Lane." He shifted in his seat so he could look at her. "Since when do you believe what they print online? Remember, those are the same fools that said we were getting married."

"Like that would ever happen."

"Exactly." His tone softened just a bit.

He didn't have to agree so quickly, like the thought of marrying her would be worse than a death sentence. Maybe it was better if they didn't talk. In fact, that sounded like a really good idea.

The ride had gone far worse than he'd imagined.

Thankfully, the Christmas party was faring much better.

Simon was certain he was losing his touch with women. That or Pepper was immune to his charms. Rekindling their friendship was never going to happen. The realization was a sobering one.

But even though their relationship was broken beyond recognition, he noticed that didn't stop her from putting on the most amazing display of pastries. But it wasn't just sweet treats. She'd mingled in flowers and twinkle lights. The display really drew the eye.

She was attentive to the guests as their hungry

gazes meandered over the lengthy selection of sugary temptations. She was kind. She was patient. And she beamed as she talked about the baked goods and her beloved bakery.

As a professional, he had no qualms with her. On a personal note, he wished they'd never taken things to the next level—even if it had been the most amazing night of his life. The price had been too high. It had cost him a friendship that he didn't know how much he valued until it'd ended.

He made his way through the great room, greeting all of his guests. These were important clients who'd helped get his products on the store shelves. And now that he was branching out with his Pet Playground chain, he was talking it up, hoping a groundswell of excitement would carry through to his launch at Christmas.

"Your Christmas tree is gorgeous," the wife of a business associate said.

"Thank you." Simon didn't admit that the tree wasn't his. His assistant had hired a decorator to come in and stage the house with holiday cheer. When the party was over, the tree, the twinkle lights and all of the other decorations would go away. None too soon as far as he was concerned.

But the funny thing was, as much as he tried

to talk business, everyone wanted to talk about the baker he'd hired. Forget the heated appetizers; they were all agog over the sweets. Not that he could blame them. They were delicious.

"Isn't she the best?" Elaine stepped up next to him.

His assistant was a few years younger than him, married and the most efficient assistant he'd ever hired. He would be lost without her. She kept him and his calendar on task.

"Yes, Pepper is very good." He only hired the best.

"The guests seem to love her. And everyone seems to be enjoying themselves."

He nodded. "You've done an excellent job coordinating this party."

He made a mental note to speak with Elaine at a later date about removing Pepper from their list of vendors. No matter how good Pepper was, they needed to maintain their distance. He felt bad about having to do it, but it was for the best—for both of their sakes. Because no matter how much they both wanted to deny it, there was still chemistry sizzling between them.

His gaze kept straying to Pepper. He assured himself that it was his job to keep an eye on the staff, to make sure the party was running smoothly. He noticed her on the phone. He couldn't have his employees chatting while they were supposed to be working. She turned her back to him and headed toward the kitchen with the phone pressed to her ear.

His jaw tightened. Surely she had to know how important this party was to him. He set off after her. When he stepped into the kitchen, the door almost bumped Pepper.

"Are you sure?" she said into the phone. "Okay. Okay. I... I'm out of town. I'll be there as soon as I can."

He couldn't see her face, but he could hear the tremor in her voice. "What's the matter?"

She turned to him. Her face was white like the frosted snowflake cookies on the buffet. Her eyes filled with unshed tears, but she didn't speak.

"What's the matter?" He repeated with more urgency.

"I have to go." She rushed to the coat check.

He followed her. "Go where?"

She attempted to shove her hand in the sleeve of her coat, but missed. She tried again and got it. Her movements were quick and jerky. She muttered something under her breath.

"What did you say?"

"My backpack. I need my backpack."

It was hanging right in front of her. He took it down from the hook. "Here you go. Now tell me, what is going on?"

"I don't have time. I have to go."

Concern pumped through his veins. He took her by the shoulders. "Pepper, look at me." When her wide-eyed stare met his, he said, "Tell me what's going on."

"The bakery. It's on fire."

"Fire?" This was the very last thing he was expecting her to say. "Are you sure?"

"It was the alarm company."

"Okay." He rushed to process this information. "Maybe it's a false alarm. Those happen all of the time."

"I have to go." She looked as though she was trying to figure out how to get around him, as he was blocking the doorway.

There was no way she was in any condition to drive. Before he could decide the right and the wrong of it, he said, "I'll take you."

"Fine. Let's go."

The fact that she didn't argue with him let him know how scared she was of losing the most important thing in her life. He texted his driver to meet them in the back. And then he texted

Elaine to let her know that she was in charge of the party, as he had an emergency.

Once they were seated in the back of the black sedan, the driver wasted no time heading south to the city. Simon wasn't sure what to do to comfort Pepper. She wrung her hands together as she stared out the window at the passing lights.

He wanted to say something—do something—to lessen her worry. "Everything will be all right."

Her head whipped around and her worried gaze met his. "You don't know that. I was certain I'd forgotten something when we left. What if it was the stove? What if I started the fire?"

He reached out, taking her hand in his and giving it a squeeze. "If that's the case, we'll deal with it."

"Everything I had—everything I dreamed about—is tied up in the bakery. What will I do? How could I be so stupid?"

"Calm down. You don't even know if anything happened."

She left her hand in his. It felt comfortable there, as though they'd been doing it for years. And though it was a small gesture, at least he was able to do something for her.

CHAPTER FOUR

RED LIGHTS FLASHED off the nearby buildings. There were emergency vehicles and people loitering everywhere. A news crew was filming in front of the bakery—or what was left of the bakery.

"This can't be happening," Pepper whispered to herself, willing herself to wake up from this nightmare.

"Pepper?" Simon's voice drew her from her troubled thoughts.

She glanced back out the window. She knew that once she stepped outside the car this horrible scene would become her reality. Her dream had quite literally gone up in smoke.

How had this happened? She'd been so careful, having the place rewired from top to bottom and having a pricey alarm system installed. She'd done everything she could think of, and still it wasn't enough.

"Pepper, if you'd rather remain here, I can go

check on things for you," Simon said in the gentlest tone.

She gave a resolute shake of her head. This was her nightmare. She should be the one to face the damage. Pepper drew in a deep breath and released an uneven sigh.

She clutched the door handle. All she could see were the flashing red lights. She had no doubt that for a long while she'd be seeing them every time she closed her eyes. She couldn't stall any longer. She had to go. She would be told what she already knew—her dream had gone up in smoke.

She wasn't sure how she got from the car and past the police officer who was keeping people back from the scene, to stand in front of her bakery. Black soot trailed up the front of the building. The air was heavy with the foul odor of smoke.

The backs of her eyes stung. All she could do was stand there, struggling to take it all in. Just a couple of hours ago she'd had a home, a business. Her heart splintered into a million pieces. Now she had nothing. Only the clothes on her back.

Her throat tightened. Her knees gave way. And then there was an arm around her waist.

Simon pulled her back against him. He held them both up.

"Let me take you back to the car," he said gently.

She shook her head, not trusting her voice. She didn't want to go anywhere.

She wasn't sure how much time had passed when a firefighter stepped up to them. "I was told the owner is here." The older man's gaze immediately moved to Simon. "Is that you?"

"Pepper owns the bakery."

She glanced at the man's helmet. It said Captain on it. To her, he was the messenger of bad news. "The bakery—is it completely burned?"

"Afraid so."

In that moment, she was thankful for Simon's support. This was like losing a member of her family...again. She'd lost her eccentric mother and her conservative grandmother. The bakery was all she had left of either of them. And now she didn't have it either.

"But there's some good news," the fire captain said. "Thanks to the fire alarm, we were able to get here fast enough to save the second story. Granted, there will be smoke damage, but it won't need the repairs the first floor will need." The man paused and looked at her as though expecting her to launch endless questions at him. "I'm really sorry, ma'am."

"How...how soon can I get in there?"

He shook his head. "It'll be a while. The fire marshal has been requested."

"The fire marshal?" Simon finally spoke.

The captain nodded. "In cases like this, he's called in to determine if this was a case of arson."

"Arson?" Pepper's eyes widened. "Who would burn down a bakery?"

The captain looked at her, but he didn't say anything. And then she realized she was now considered a suspect—torching her own place for the insurance money. She was certain it wasn't a secret that her bakery was struggling now that the chain store had moved in.

The fire captain seemed to size her up with his gaze. He was trying to figure out if she had it in her to burn down the place.

"Stop looking at me like that. I didn't do this. I would never do this." Her voice was rising and people were starting to turn in their direction. "I'm not an arsonist. Go find who did this! It's not me! It's not me!"

"Let's go," Simon said calmly.

"I don't want to go until he stops looking at me like I'm some criminal."

"Maybe just a little space will help."

She looked at Simon. "Do I look like a criminal to you?"

With his arm still around her waist, Simon directed her away from the bakery. "You look beautiful to me."

Any other time, his compliment would have stirred something within her, but right now there was nothing but torment, angst and grief. There was no room for good feelings. Life as she knew it was over—again.

Why did she keep losing the things and people that meant the most to her?

Her head started to pound and her stomach churned. The rest of it was a blur, until she was once again sitting in the back of Simon's car. They were rushing down the street and she had no idea where they were going. It wasn't like she had anywhere to go.

"Here." Simon pressed a bottle into her hand. "Drink it."

She glanced at the bottle and then at him.

"It's water. Drink it. You look like you're ready to pass out."

Her gaze searched his. "Tell me this is a nightmare. Tell me that when I wake up it will be over."

"I wish I could."

Her bottom lip trembled.

"My beautiful bakery. It's gone." Her voice cracked. "It's all gone."

Was this shock? She'd heard people talk about out-of-body experiences. Was that what was happening to her?

"Do you want me to take you to the hospital?" Simon asked. The concern was evident on his face.

"The hospital? Why? I wasn't in the fire."

"For shock. This can't be easy for you."

She had to pull it together. She'd been doing fine on her own. She couldn't let a fire undo her. She was made of sturdier stuff than that; at least that's what her grandmother used to always tell her when she missed her mother. The Kane women were made of sturdy stuff. They could get through anything.

Pepper glanced at the water. She didn't want it, but she knew if she didn't pull herself together that they would be at the ER posthaste. And that was one more bill she didn't need.

She pressed the bottle to her dry lips. The cool liquid soothed her scratchy throat. She drank half the bottle. After handing it back to him, she leaned back against the black leather upholstery and closed her eyes.

With her eyes still closed, she asked, "Where are we going?"

"Do you have someplace to go? A relative?"

She shook her head. "There's just me."

"A boyfriend?"

Her eyes sprang open and narrowed in on him. "After my last brief but disastrous romantic encounter, I haven't bothered with dating."

Simon's mouth opened, but then he seemed to decide it was best not to say anything at this particular juncture, and his lips pressed together in a firm line.

Good. Because on top of the fire, she didn't have the energy to argue with him.

"Just let me out here." Why was she telling Simon? It wasn't like he was driving the car. She leaned forward, speaking to the driver, "If you could pull over, I'd appreciate it."

The driver didn't say anything. But she could see his gaze in the rearview mirror moving to Simon with a question in his eyes.

Simon shook his head.

Pepper huffed out an indignant breath. "Simon, what are you doing? You can't just kidnap me."

"I'm not. I'm being your friend. You had a huge shock tonight and I'm worried about you. Until I'm sure you're okay and have a safe place to go, I'm going to keep an eye on you."

If he expected her to be grateful, she wasn't. She was… She was full of pent-up anger. It was like the world was out to get her. Every time she found happiness, the rug somehow got ripped out from under her.

And she was taking all her frustration out on Simon. He watched her with concern in his eyes. And rightfully so. She was acting strangely. And she was pretty certain they were nearing the hospital.

Get it together, Pepper.

"I have to go back. I have to look after the bakery," her voice wavered, "My home."

"I'll take care of it." He withdrew his phone from his pocket and made a brief phone call. "Your building will be secured."

She wondered what it was like to make problems disappear with a mere phone call. If only that's all it took to right all that had gone wrong in her life.

She took a moment to steady her rising emotions. "Where are we going?"

"To my place."

She shook her head. "I can't go back there with all of your guests. I couldn't possibly face them."

"Don't worry. We're not going back to Connecticut. We're going to stay right here in the city. Home, James."

The car slowed at the next intersection and turned away from the hospital that was now only a block away. Thank goodness. If it came down to facing a bunch of doctors or facing her ex, if she could call him that, she would pick Simon. She wasn't sure it was the smartest choice, but it seemed like the simplest at that moment.

The fight had gone out of her, to the point where he feared she might very well collapse. On the ride up in the elevator, he kept a steady arm around her waist, pulling her weight against him.

Once inside his penthouse, he thought of getting her a drink. Something strong to take the edge off. But he didn't know what sort of alcohol she drank or even if she drank at all. And then a thought came to him. It was something his mother used to do for him when he was very young and too worked up to sleep after a run-in with his father.

He led Pepper toward the kitchen. She didn't question where they were going. She simply let him lead the way. If this kept up much longer, he was following through with his initial instinct to take her to the ER.

"Here." He guided her to one of the stools at the center island. "Sit down."

She did it without a fuss.

He hesitated to move from her side, afraid without him next to her that she would collapse. But she held her own and sat there, staring blindly ahead.

"I'm just going to get you something warm to drink." For all intents and purposes, he was talking to himself.

There were just a couple of things he did well in the kitchen. And this happened to be one of them. He set to work.

A couple minutes later, with a warm mug in hand, he turned to Pepper. She looked dazed and lost. Deciding she'd be much more comfortable in one of his guest rooms, he moved to her side.

"How about we make you comfortable?" When she finally looked at him, he asked, "Can you stand?"

She did so without a word.

Together, they made their way to the guest room with the king-size bed. He guided her to it. She sat down on the edge.

He held out the mug. "Here. Have a drink."

She shook her head. Still no words.

He knelt down in front of her and gazed up at her. Her eyes shimmered with unshed tears. That had to be a good sign. Right? Something was going on inside of her. Now if he could just get her to talk.

He lifted the mug. "Go ahead. Have some."

Her gaze moved from him to the mug. "What is it?"

He let out his first full breath since her meltdown back at the bakery. "It's hot chocolate. It's what I used to drink when I was little and had a hard time going to sleep. This is good, but it isn't my secret recipe. I didn't have time to make it tonight, but I promise to make it for you some other time."

She reached for the cup. When her fingers brushed his, he noticed how cold she was. While she drank the hot chocolate, he grabbed a fluffy white throw blanket from the bottom of the bed. He draped it around her shoulders.

She set the cup on the nightstand and leaned back against the headboard. He slipped off her shoes, setting them at the foot of the bed. When he glanced up at her, he noticed her swiping away the tears.

He sat on the edge of the bed. He hated this feeling of helplessness. It was a position he wasn't used to being in. Pepper looked so fragile, as though a breeze could scatter the pieces that made her whole.

He swallowed hard. "Can I get you anything?"

Silence was the only answer.

There had to be something—anything that he could do to help her. He assured himself that it was nothing more than he would feel for a stranger in a similar situation.

"I was thinking—" her soft voice broke through his thoughts "—that I can't remember what we talked about the last time...the last time we had coffee together at the bakery."

He didn't say a word for a moment. This was what she wanted to talk about? With her world crumbling around her, she wanted to talk about them?

He knew it wasn't a good idea to go strolling down memory lane. In fact, it was a very dangerous path laced with emotional bombs that could go off at any time. But at least she was communicating with him. He just wasn't sure how to respond to her.

"I know we talked about a lot of things over the months," she said. "Those early morning coffees were so cozy because no customers ventured in quite that early. It was my favorite time of the day. It was my chance to enjoy the bakery instead of worrying about producing all of the orders for the day. In those early morning hours before the sunrise, everything held such promise. And the bakery was filled with the most amazing aromas from the fresh baked goods." She inhaled deeply as though in her mind she could still smell them instead of the lingering scent of smoke that seemed to follow them around.

He should probably say something here. But these were Pepper's precious memories and he didn't want to say anything to sully them. So he sat by quietly as she took them both back in time to that very special bakery.

She fidgeted with a loose thread on the throw blanket while averting her gaze. "I looked forward to your Wednesday morning visits. I'd tuck away in my mind all of the interesting things that had happened since we last met, just so I'd have something to talk to you about. Each time we parted, it was just until the next time. I never thought there wouldn't be a next time. And now I've been trying to remember the last time we shared coffee at the bakery…" Her voice cracked.

His mind rewound back in time. He remembered everything about her, from the way she fidgeted with the silver necklace when she was nervous to the way her smiles would light up her emerald green eyes. He'd quickly learned that Pepper was someone he would never forget. No matter how much he tried.

"I was late that morning." His gaze met hers, hoping he was doing the right thing. "You were wearing an orange, green and red polka-dotted apron. You called it your autumn apron. And you were all excited because you'd just perfected a new recipe."

As he spoke, she relaxed against the pillows. He longed to reach out and smooth away the strawberry blond curls that rested against her pale cheek. But he didn't want to frighten her off. She'd had enough turmoil for one evening. And so he kept his hands to himself while doing his best to comfort her with his words.

Still, his chest ached for her and all she'd lost that night. That bakery had been so much more than her job. It had been her life. And he ached for the very special friendship that he'd ruined with one night of passion. By letting go of his common sense and following his desires, he'd lost a dear friend. Pepper had been someone who was so easy to be around. She wasn't pushy and she wasn't needy. She was warm and understanding. Sometimes they'd just sit quietly, drinking their coffees and watching as the first morning rays filled the sky.

He clearly recalled the softness of her laughter. Oh, how he missed how her eyes would light up. And he missed how she would tease him about being a workaholic, which he'd often turn around on her, as she worked as many hours as him, if not more.

As her gaze prodded him for more details, he said, "I remember not having time to sit and talk that morning because I was running late. I'd been up most of the night before brainstorming an idea for the Pet Playground. I had a meeting to get to and you had a special order to bake. But we paused at the counter long enough to agree to go out and celebrate after I launched my chain of stores and you added a new line of cakes."

Her eyes lit up as though the memories were starting to come back to her. "The new recipe was a carrot caramel cake. It was going to be a signature cake."

He nodded. "It was moist and delicious. When

I went to leave, you stepped out from behind the counter and handed me a box of pastries for the office. I caught a whiff of your perfume." He inhaled deeply, as he had that day. "It was a soft floral fragrance."

"Lavender." She settled further down on the pillows. Her eyes looked heavy.

He thought about it for a moment and then nodded. "The scent works for you."

He couldn't help but wonder if he were to lean forward, if she would smell of lavender. Instead, he remained perfectly still.

"Those were good times." Her voice grew softer as utter exhaustion hit her.

"They were the best." He stood.

"I don't know what I'm going to do." Though her voice was barely above a whisper, he could still hear the raw pain.

Sympathy welled up in him. This shouldn't have happened to her. Pepper was the sweetest, kindest soul. She deserved only the best in life. It was probably the reason she'd dumped him as soon as he'd let down his guard with her. Beneath the stylish haircut and the expensive clothes, he was a damaged soul.

He gave himself a mental shake. This wasn't

the time to consider himself. Right now, Pepper needed all his attention.

As a tear trickled down her cheek, he gently swiped it away. "Shh… Just rest for tonight."

"Tomorrow…" Her eyes closed.

Tomorrow would come too soon for both of them. Tomorrow she would have to relive the pain of loss all over again. And he would once again experience that helpless feeling. But that was then and this was now.

He retrieved another blanket from the closet and laid it over her. She was still fully dressed and that couldn't be comfortable to sleep in, but he wasn't going to disturb her. The fact she was sleeping was miracle enough. He hoped in her sleep she was able to escape the nasty reality of her life. He wished for her the sweetest dreams.

He stopped next to her. A strand of hair lay across her face. He reached out, moving it to the side. She didn't stir.

It was then that he noticed the tear tracks on her pale cheeks. Sympathy welled up in his chest. He bent over and placed a gentle kiss to her forehead. If only he knew how to make this better for her…

He reached for the switch on the bedside light. His hand paused in midair. If she were to suddenly wake up, she would most likely be disoriented. But the constant glare of the light might stir her from some much-needed rest. In the end, he turned it off, hoping she would sleep through the night. He walked softly to the doorway. He paused and glanced back. She hadn't moved at all. She was out cold.

As he moved toward the master suite, he couldn't help but recall their early morning chats. If he didn't know better, he'd have sworn she'd taken him down memory lane just to torture him. But he knew she wasn't a vengeful person. Tonight, she'd just needed the comfort she found in those memories.

When the sun rose and reality settled in for both of them, it would be quite apparent that too much had happened for them to go back in time and rekindle that friendship. She could stay until other reasonable arrangements could be made, which should be as soon as the insurance company released funds for temporary lodging.

Until that time, he would keep his distance. It was best for both of them.

But just in case Pepper awoke during the night and needed anything, he left his bedroom door ajar. After changing out of his clothes, he lay in the dark. He stared at the ceiling because he knew sleep would be illusive. Sure enough, his thoughts of Pepper kept him awake long into the night.

CHAPTER FIVE

HE WAS WORRIED.

Maybe they should have gone to the hospital last night.

The following morning, Simon was sitting in the living room at ten o'clock. He'd had his first, second and third cup of coffee. He'd skipped his routine of going to the gym because he wanted to be around in case Pepper needed anything. And she still hadn't roused.

Should he go check on her? After all, he did say he was going to keep an eye on her. Wasn't it his responsibility to make sure she was fine?

He folded the morning paper that he'd skimmed without really noticing anything on the page. He kept thinking of Pepper and remembering her look of utter devastation. He'd never seen anyone look so distraught. He couldn't blame her. He knew how much she cared about the bakery. She was handling the loss far better than he would have should he ever lose Ross Toys.

He moved silently along the hallway toward the guest room. He paused. There were no sounds coming from inside. Maybe she was still sleeping. He glanced at his wristwatch. He doubted it. She was an early riser just like him.

It's one of the reasons they'd become friends over this past year. And since the paparazzi debacle, he had really missed their friendship. He hadn't realized just how much he looked forward to their early morning chats over coffee and a pastry in the wee hours before the bakery filled with people.

Because he'd let his guard down—because he'd allowed himself to get caught up in the moment—he'd lost someone who treated him like a normal person instead of like a boss or a rich man or an eligible bachelor. To Pepper, he'd just been a friendly face. And maybe it was selfish of him, but he wanted that friendship back. Would she be willing to give him another chance?

He raised his knuckles to the door.

Tap. Tap.

He waited. No response.

Tap. Tap. Tap.

"Pepper?"

Still no response.

He was really starting to worry.

His hand moved toward the door handle. He hesitated. Something could be wrong with her. Or perhaps she'd left during the night and was meandering the streets. The thought twisted his gut with worry.

Or maybe she was in the shower. Or perhaps she hadn't slept well and was finally dozing. And it wasn't like they hadn't spent the night together and he hadn't seen her in bed. Still, a lot had changed since that night. In fact, everything had changed.

"I'm coming in," he called out. He eased the door open slowly. "Pepper?"

Silence.

He stuck his head inside the room. He immediately spotted the empty bed and disheveled covers. At least she had gotten some rest.

Just then the door to the en suite opened. Pepper's surprised gaze met his. But it wasn't her reaction to him being in her room that bothered him, it was her pale face.

"Simon, what are you doing in here?"

"Sorry. I knocked. I knocked a lot. And when you didn't respond, I started to worry that you might not feel well."

"I… I'm fine."

He searched her face. He could tell she was

lying, but he didn't dare accuse her. Instead, he would pretend everything was fine, which clearly it wasn't. But until he figured out what he could do to help her, it was best to play it safe.

"Can I get you something to eat? Eggs? Toast? Waffles? Or pancakes?"

At that, Pepper's face turned about three shades of green. She held up a finger indicating he should wait. Then the bathroom door slammed shut. What in the world?

As he approached the door, he knew what was the matter. Pepper didn't feel well. It was the shock from last night. He couldn't blame her. If his business was to suddenly go up in flames, he would be utterly devastated too. But she just had to realize that this was just a temporary setback, not the end.

Unless…unless she didn't have insurance. He couldn't imagine not having insurance, but he also knew when money was tight, corners were cut. If that was the case, it just might be the end. No wonder she felt so poorly.

He wasn't sure what to do. He didn't want to make matters worse, so he moved to the doorway and waited. A few minutes later, the bathroom door opened. Pepper stood there. Even her lips were pale this time.

He rushed over to her. "Maybe you should sit down."

She didn't say anything or put up a fight as he guided her to the side of the bed. She must feel as bad as she looked.

"Stay here. I'll be right back."

He rushed to the kitchen. He knew his house-keeper/cook kept it well stocked. He was about to find out just how well stocked. The pantry was not a place he ventured very often, but when he opened the door, he was quite pleased with the selection.

He quickly located a can of ginger ale. And then he moved to the fridge. Recalling what his mother used to give him when his stomach was upset, he toasted some bread and served it plain.

He returned to the room to find Pepper had made the bed and was straightening the place. He was shocked she was up and about. She hadn't looked well enough to do any of this. And she was still looking ill.

"You don't have to do that," he said.

"Of course I do." Then she frowned. "You're right. I should strip the bed in order to wash the linens."

He was horrified that she thought she had to come here and do the laundry. "Pepper, come over here." He gestured to a small table in front of the window. When she didn't move, he said, "I pay people to take care of things like changing the bed and washing the laundry. You are my guest. And you don't feel good. You need to take it easy. You had quite a shock last night."

She sighed and moved to the table. She sat down and looked at the things he'd brought her, but she didn't make any motion to eat or drink.

"It's ginger ale and some plain toast," he said, sitting across from her. "My, uh, mother used to give it to me when I didn't feel good. I thought it might help you. But if you prefer something else—"

"No. This is fine." And then her gaze met his. "Thank you for being so thoughtful. And I'm sorry about everything, from tearing you away from your party to making a scene last night and then putting you out—"

"Stop. You don't have to be sorry about anything. To be honest, that party was boring. It was a bunch of people who wanted to be seen."

"Then why did you host it?"

"Because it was expected."

She studied him. "So you did it because people expected you to do it, even though you, personally, didn't enjoy it."

"Something like that. But enough about me. What can I do to help you?"

"You were helping me."

"I was?" He didn't follow her meaning.

She nodded. "By talking about yourself and your party for just a few brief seconds, I was able to think about something besides the nightmare that is now my life."

"Oh." He wasn't used to talking about himself. In fact, he made it a point to share as little as possible, because whatever he told people eventually ended up on some tabloid site.

But Pepper was different. He'd told her a lot about himself and none of it had ended up on any gossip sites. All their morning chat sessions had been kept private.

And even after their night together, when things had gone terribly wrong, she still hadn't turned to the tabloids and vented. Was it wrong that he'd braced himself for that exact eventuality? How could he have doubted Pepper's character? She was exactly what she seemed—a wonderful, caring person.

The events of last night felt like a nightmare.

The problem was, when she woke up this morning, it was all real.

With her stomach now settled, Pepper was on the subway headed toward her bakery. Wearing the same clothes she'd had on yesterday, she sat on the bench as her stop quickly approached.

Soon she would be back at the bakery—or what was left of it. She wrung her hands together. She was hoping in the light of day that the damage would be less than she imagined. Maybe it was just a small stove fire that could be quickly and easily remedied. Could she be that lucky?

She didn't consider herself a lucky person. Everything she'd gained in life she'd worked for, or it had come with a very dear price. Her thoughts turned to the loss of her grandmother and the modest inheritance she'd received. At first, she hadn't wanted to take the money. It just felt wrong to take her grandmother's money and roll it into her dream of a bakery.

And then she'd received a letter from her grandmother's attorney. Her grandmother had written her a short but pointed letter, basically ordering Pepper to follow her dreams. It was so like her grandmother to propel her forward into the unknown, because nothing was gained without taking chances.

But now it had all gone up in smoke. The

thought weighed heavy on her heart. She had no idea where to go from here. She definitely needed a plan ASAP.

She couldn't believe Simon had cared for her. She must have been a pathetic mess, for him to take her home last night. She knew the only reason he would take her in would be pity. Because she knew without a doubt that he had absolutely no feelings for her.

It was nice that he'd lingered around the penthouse that morning to make sure she was feeling better and over the shock of the fire. He'd left before her, but she didn't waste much time. She had to find somewhere to live besides Simon's place. She hoped that it would be back in her apartment.

She exited the subway and made her way toward Mulberry Street. It wasn't far from here. Light flurries fell from the sky, melting as the snow hit the sidewalk. Normally, she'd enjoy the wintery scene, but today she was too distraught to find the beauty in anything.

Her feet felt heavy as she walked. Her steps weren't as quick as they'd normally be. All the while, she tried to prepare herself for what she might see, but how did one prepare for the end of a dream?

As she turned the corner, she caught her first glimpse of the bakery. There was yellow caution tape up around it. Pepper barely noticed the people she passed on the sidewalk or the cars rushing up the road. Her sole focus was on the bakery.

And then she stopped across the street from it. Her heart clenched. Her beautiful bakery was a broken, sooty mess. Tears stung the back of her eyes. She blinked them away. She'd fallen apart last night, but today she had to keep it together. She had to formulate a plan.

She hesitated. She stood there taking in the boarded-up display window and the stripes of soot running up the white painted brick. The black awning seemed to have fared okay. She crossed the street, finding it was only an illusion. Upon closer inspection, she could see the toll the fire had taken on the material. It would need replacing.

It might be a mess, but the bakery was still standing. That had to be a good sign. A glimmer of hope flickered within her. Was it possible to rebuild her beloved bakery?

She moved to the door. There was a sign on it, but she didn't pause to read it. She was anxious to get inside and see what needed to be done.

Her hand touched the door handle just as it was pulled open. A tall man in a firefighter's jacket stood there. His expression was serious as he frowned at her.

"You can't be here. Didn't you read the sign?"

"But I own the bakery."

He nodded. "You still can't be here."

"But I live here." All she had were the clothes on her back. "I need to get to my things."

"That's not going to happen. The fire marshal hasn't been here to do his report yet."

"What report?"

He didn't answer her as he stepped outside, forcing her to back up on the sidewalk. The man was so tall that she couldn't see around him to get a glimpse of the inside.

The man eyed her as though making up his mind about her. "There's a suspicion of arson."

"Arson?"

In the back of her mind, she vaguely remembered arson being mentioned the night before. The memories were blurry. But by the way this man was looking at her, he thought she was guilty.

The bakery was as bad as he remembered.

Simon had just had a look at the back of the

building, since no one would allow him inside. He'd been hoping the fire was minor and Pepper could return home today, but it wasn't going to happen. That much was evident from the outside. He could only imagine the damage to the inside.

He thought of Pepper and another wave of sympathy came over him. The fire last night had hit her so hard that he wasn't sure how she was going to take the sight of her bakery all charred. It didn't even slightly resemble the trendy bakery that it'd been a mere twenty-four hours ago.

He rounded the building and stopped on the sidewalk in front of the bakery as he spotted Pepper. The short-tempered fire captain that he'd had the misfortune of running into was now walking away from her. That man was definitely not the friendliest guy. His words were short and blunt.

When Simon had tried to get inside to eyeball the damage, he'd been told no. There was no room for discussion. The captain didn't care who Simon was, and that was fair enough, but the man provided absolutely no information that would help Pepper. None whatsoever. And so Simon had to wonder what the man was holding back.

He focused his attention on Pepper. His jaw tightened when he saw the distressed look on her face. He was certain the captain had done nothing to help matters.

Simon approached her. "Are you okay?"

She shook her head. "Have you seen this place?" And then she moved her distraught gaze to him. "What are you doing here? Shouldn't you be at the office?"

"I wanted to see where things stood."

"Don't worry." Her eyes reflected her pain. "I'll be out of your penthouse as soon as I contact the insurance company."

"There's no rush." He instinctively reached out to her, drawing her near. Initially, she resisted, but then she let herself be drawn into a hug.

There on the sidewalk, with flurries swirling around them, they stood wrapped in each other's arms. Holding her close drove home how much he'd truly missed her—missed everything about her.

He murmured against her hair, "You can stay as long as you need."

She pulled away, and with great reluctance, he let her go. "I'll make other arrangements. You've done too much already."

Perhaps it was best to change the subject. "What did the fire captain say to you?"

"That I couldn't get inside." Her fine brows drew together. "Did he let you inside?"

Simon shook his head. "He's a very unfriendly guy."

"That's what I thought. I tried to tell him that I live here and I needed to get to my stuff—especially my clothes. He didn't care."

"Hopefully, you'll be able to get inside soon. Can I give you a lift back to the penthouse?"

She shook her head. "I have some shopping I need to do."

"Can I drop you anywhere?"

Again, she shook her head. "It isn't far and I feel like walking."

He watched her walk away, wondering if he should go with her. Something told him if he tried, she'd refuse his company. At least she had his phone number. If she needed anything, she could call him. But would she?

CHAPTER SIX

AND THE HITS kept coming.

The insurance company refused to release the funds until arson was ruled out.

Pepper couldn't believe she was suspected of arson. Her. A person who loved her little bakery with all her heart. A person who was lost without her warm kitchen filled with scents of cinnamon, apples, cherries and a bunch of buttery goodness.

Not sure what to tell Simon, she took advantage of his invitation to make herself at home in his penthouse. So after a quick stop at the grocery store, she made her way to Simon's massive kitchen. She lost herself in her baking. It was cathartic for her.

And then it was time to head to the animal shelter where she volunteered at least once a week, sometimes it was more. Next to her bakery, it was where she was most comfortable. And until the renovations were complete, Pepper looked forward to her visits to the Helping Paw Shelter each weekend. She carried in the boxes of cookies, cupcakes and Danishes for the adopt-a-pet event.

"Pepper, I didn't think you'd be able to make it." Stephanie, the assistant director of the shelter, rushed over and gave her a hug. "We heard about the fire, and I'm so sorry. Is there anything I can do?"

"Thank you. I appreciate the offer, but there's nothing to do right now but wait for all of the paperwork to get done." She didn't want to discuss the arson investigation.

"How bad was it?"

Images of the scorched front of the bakery flashed through her mind. "It looks bad from the outside."

"What about the inside? What about your apartment?"

Pepper shook her head. "I don't know. They won't let me inside yet."

"Oh, Pepper, that's awful. Where are you staying?"

"With a friend." Heat rushed to her face when she thought of Simon. She didn't know if he still qualified as a friend, but she didn't know what else to call him.

A smile eased the worried look on Stephanie's face. "Must be a guy friend."

Her body grew increasingly warm. "Why would you say that?"

"Because you're blushing. Tell me it's Simon Ross."

"Shh…" Pepper glanced around to make sure they weren't overheard.

"It is." Stephanie grinned and quietly clapped her hands. "How did this happen?"

Pepper needed someone to talk to about the events of her life and Stephanie had become a good friend. She gave her a brief overview of the events of the last twenty-four hours.

"Wow. I can't believe all of that happened to you."

"Me either." Her thoughts turned to the problems with the insurance company. "I don't know what I'm going to do."

"I'd offer to let you stay with me, but all I have is a lumpy couch. It's yours if you want it though."

"Thanks. I'll keep it in mind."

Stephanie checked the time. "Let's get a table set up for all of your goodies."

Pepper glanced around and noticed that nothing for the event was set out. They must have thought she wasn't coming. "I should have called to let you know I could still make it. And I have some goodies for the four-footed little ones." Lately, she'd started baking doggie biscuits and experimenting with kitty treats.

"You know, they like them so much that you should consider starting your own pet line." Stephanie's gaze moved to all the baked goods. "I can't believe you baked all of this, considering everything that just happened to you."

"It felt good to bake. I might have made a little too much."

"Never. It'll all be gone by the end of the evening."

Pepper set up the table with the pastries she'd brought with her. "You really think so?"

"I do." She glanced up at the clock. "We have a little time before the adoption party. Come with me."

Pepper glanced back at the table that wasn't totally set up. She really should stay here. She needed it to look its best. Even though her bakery was temporarily out of business, she was not giving up. She intended to use the insurance money to fix everything and then life would go back to normal. In the meantime, she was passing out her business cards in hopes that people would call her for cakes and remember the name of her bakery and come to visit when she had her grand reopening.

"You can do that later," Stephanie said. "I have someone for you to meet."

Meet? Pepper wondered who it could be. She'd been coming to the shelter for so long that she knew all the volunteers by name. Maybe they'd taken on someone new.

Pepper followed Stephanie to the back of the shelter where they housed the puppies. Each doggie looked so sweet to Pepper. They all had their sad stories that pulled at Pepper's heart strings. If it were up to her, she'd adopt them all. If only she had a big enough house and all of the hours necessary to care for them.

She did take care of foster dogs from time to time. They were usually very special cases. However, with the opening of the bakery, she hadn't had the free time that she used to.

Stephanie led her to the last kennel and stopped. "Pepper, I'd like you to meet Daisy."

Inside the kennel was a beagle puppy. She was timid and smashed herself against the back corner. She was the most adorable fur baby with her brown, floppy ears. Pepper's heart immediately melted.

"What happened?" she asked.

"We don't know the details. Only that someone found the puppies in a box in the freezing cold. Daisy was the only one to make it. However, she isn't ready for adoption yet. She has a lot of recovery to do. And as you can tell, she needs to be socialized. She doesn't trust people, and with her history, I can't blame her."

"Can I try?" Pepper was drawn to the puppy.

"Go ahead. I don't have to tell you to take it slow."

No, she didn't. Pepper had done this countless times. She opened the kennel door. "Hey, Daisy. My name's Pepper." She wanted the puppy to get used to her voice. "I was hoping we could be friends."

Daisy silently stared at her with those big brown eyes. Her whole body, from her nose to the tip of her tail, quivered with fear. She was going to be a tough case, but Pepper was eager to work with her. Immediately, Pepper felt a bond forming between them.

In one breath, she knew she wanted to take Daisy home. In the next breath, she remembered the sobering fact that she didn't have a home. And Pepper was quite certain that Simon would not appreciate having a puppy on his gleaming floors or near his priceless pieces of art. To Pepper, it was like the man lived in a museum rather than a home.

"I'll just let you two get acquainted," Stephanie said with a knowing smile.

A while ago, Pepper had mentioned that she would love to have a beagle. Leave it to Stephanie to remember. But she was not adopting Daisy. She was in absolutely no position to even consider it.

Pepper reached into her pocket and pulled out the doggie biscuits she'd made. They were all too big for the little girl. "I'm sorry," Pepper said, "I don't have any treats for puppies. We don't have too many puppies your size that pass through here. But I promise to make you some for our next visit."

Pepper stayed there visiting with Daisy for as long as she dared before going to finish setting up the table. And then she took a seat at the information desk, where she was assigned to work for the next few hours.

She was tired. Absolutely exhausted.

It felt as though she hadn't slept in days.

Pepper used the spare key Simon had given her to let herself into the penthouse. All she wanted now was to curl up with a black-and-white classic movie—

"You're home."

Pepper jumped at the sound of Simon's voice. She dropped her things near the door, then followed the voice to the living room. Simon stood next to the wall of windows overlooking Central Park.

"Did you need something?" she asked.

"I didn't know where you were, and when I couldn't reach you on the phone, I, uh, didn't know what to think, with you not feeling well this morning."

She pulled her phone out of her back pocket. The missed calls appeared on the screen. He hadn't called once. He'd called twice.

Was he worried about her? Really? Simon Ross had been worried that something had happened to her?

For the briefest moment, she toyed with the idea that he still cared—that they were still good friends. And then she dismissed the ridiculous notion. He was most likely hoping she'd found other accommodations.

She had a tiny amount in her savings. It wouldn't tide her over for long, but she didn't have much choice.

"Sorry. I had my phone on Mute. I'm feeling better now. Nothing to worry about." She thought about telling him that she'd been at the animal shelter, but she decided they weren't back at the stage where they were sharing things with each other. "Before I go, can I get you something to eat?" It seemed like such a small way to repay him for all he'd done for her, but at the moment it was all she had to offer.

He shook his head. "I'm not hungry."

"Then I'll get my things and leave."

He pressed his hands to his sides. "Where will you be staying? You know, in case something comes up and I need to reach you."

What would come up that he'd need to reach her? She refrained from posing the question. Instead, she mentioned checking into a small motel in New Jersey.

He frowned. "Surely your insurance can do better than that."

"They aren't paying. I should get going before it gets late." She turned to walk away, hoping he wouldn't ask more questions—questions she didn't want to answer.

"Why aren't they paying? You do have insurance, don't you?"

She turned back to him and shrugged her

shoulders. "I do. But there's a suspicion of arson. And until it's resolved, they've put a hold on the money."

"That's not right. If they knew you, they'd know you would never do such a thing."

It felt good to know that he was in her corner, believing in her innocence. "But that's the thing—they don't know me." She worried her bottom lip. "What if it was arson? How will I ever prove that it wasn't me?"

Sympathy glinted in his eyes as he approached her. "Don't worry. It'll all work out. And soon you'll have your bakery back."

"But not in time."

"In time?" His brows drew together.

"For all of the holiday events I had scheduled."

"I'm sure you'll get plenty of orders once you've reopened."

She wished she felt as confident as he sounded. "Only time will tell."

She turned and headed for her room. It wouldn't take long to pack her things. She had a bag of clothes she'd just purchased and that was it.

Tomorrow she'd have to start canceling her remaining list of events that she had scheduled. No matter what happened with the arson investigation, there was no way the bakery would be open and ready for operation.

Knock. Knock.

She hadn't closed her door. She turned to find Simon standing there. His forehead was creased as though he had something on his mind.

When he didn't say anything, she asked, "Did you want something?"

He nodded. "I want you to stay."

Her heart leapt into her throat. What was he saying? Had she heard him correctly? Surely not. It had been a really long day.

"What did you say?"

He stepped further into the room. With each step he took, her heart beat faster. For just a moment, she imagined him sweeping her into his arms and passionately kissing her like he'd done on that not-so-long-ago night. She missed him, his embrace, his mouth against hers—

"I'd like you to stay." His voice startled her from her wayward thoughts. "You know, until your apartment is ready. You can use the kitchen to bake. It's not like I ever use it."

She struggled not to stare at his inviting mouth—to remember the delicious things he could do to her with it. What was wrong with her? They came from very different worlds.

They obviously wanted different things in life. So why was she still drawn to him? Why did she long for him in her dreams?

Oblivious to her inner turmoil, Simon said, "I'll go order dinner while you unpack."

"Wait," she called out. "Why would you do that? Why would you want me here?" And then another more troublesome thought came to mind—troublesome from the standpoint that she didn't trust herself around him. "We aren't going to share a bed."

"No. That was a one-time thing."

His brush-off stung. It put an immediate end to her heated thoughts. Not that she wanted to pick things up where they'd left off. Still, she'd thought that night had been special for not just her. Obviously, she'd been wrong.

She told herself it was for the best; everyone and everything she cared for was eventually lost to her. She couldn't lose anyone or anything else. She was better off on her own.

"Won't my staying here be awkward?"

"I work long hours. I'm not seeing anyone. So you'll have the place to yourself most of the time. Now, I'll go order dinner."

And with that he turned and walked away like it was all settled because he said so. Part of her wanted to stay. Though this place was a bit on the cold, minimalist side, it was clean. She knew on her budget the cleanliness of the motels she could afford would be iffy at best. But why would any of that matter to Simon?

She followed him into the kitchen, where he'd just disconnected a phone call. His motives shouldn't matter to her, but they did. She tried to tell herself it was idle curiosity, nothing more.

"I hope you don't mind pepperoni pizza," he said.

"It's fine. But I can't accept your offer to stay here. It's too much. I could never repay you. You've already done so much."

He sighed. "The food is ordered. You have to eat. And it's getting late. Stay the night and think about it."

What would one more night hurt? It would certainly help stretch her funds. But she had to do something for him in return.

"I could bake you something to take to the office. Perhaps some cherry turnovers."

He didn't say anything at first, but a spark of interest shone in his eyes. "It's a deal."

Not exactly an even exchange—far from it— but at least she could hold her head up.

CHAPTER SEVEN

HE HAD A very important meeting.

It was about his company's expansion.

Simon bounded out of bed, ready to take on the world. The plan was to kick off the new line of stores right before Christmas with a shop here in New York, and then after Christmas, they would start unveiling the chain in various large cities throughout the country. But something just wasn't right.

As he grabbed a quick shower, he mulled over his uneasiness with the project. It had been bothering Simon for months. There was something lacking from their plans, that extra oomph to take their Pet Playground from okay to amazing. They didn't want to be just another pet store. They needed it to be a destination. They needed to offer something shoppers couldn't get anywhere else.

He'd had his team working on it for months. And so far, they'd come up with some good ideas, but nothing to wow him. And now their first store was about to be revealed without the wow factor. If he didn't do something fast, the new chain would sink before it even launched.

And he wouldn't let that happen.

But in the back of his mind, his father's harsh words echoed. *"You're a loser. You'll always be a loser."*

It wasn't the only time his father had spewed such hurtful words, but those were the final words his father had ever said as he was led in handcuffs from the courtroom. Ever since, Simon had strived to prove the man wrong—to prove to himself that he wasn't anything like the man with whom he shared DNA.

Simon sighed, closed his eyes and shook his head, chasing away the troubling thoughts. The ghosts of the past weren't worth dwelling on. He had more important things to do—lots of things that required his full attention.

He opened his eyes, focusing on the here and now. He dressed and headed for the kitchen. When he stepped through the doorway, he expected to find Pepper already busy baking up some wonderful smelling creations. Or decorating something she'd baked the evening before. But when he stepped into the room, there weren't any lights on. The kitchen was empty.

Where was Pepper? She'd told him the night before how much work she had to do today for the party this evening. She'd even asked how early she could start in the kitchen without disturbing him. So where was she?

He headed for her room.

Tap. Tap.

"Pepper?"

"Come in." Her voice sounded weak. It definitely lacked her usual pep.

He opened the door to find her in bed. He didn't have to ask her to know that she didn't feel well, again. This was the second day in a row. And she didn't seem to be getting any better.

He could understand the first day, with the shock of the fire. But two days due to shock with no improvement? He wasn't buying it. There was something more afoot.

"Get dressed," he said, pulling his phone from his pocket. "You're going to the doctor."

"What? No. I'll be fine. Just give me a bit. I promised to bake the items for the office—"

"Forget the baking." He shook his head. "You're not well. And this has been going on too long. I want a doctor to have a look at you and make sure it's nothing serious."

Pepper jumped out of bed. "See? I'm—"

Her face grew pale and she rushed to the bathroom. She sent the door slamming shut behind her.

Fine. Right. And I'm Santa Claus.

He pulled up the number of his family doctor. The man may be old now, but he'd been treating Simon his whole life. He wouldn't trust anyone else with Pepper.

By the time he got off the phone, having arranged an appointment right away, Pepper had returned from the bathroom. "I'm fine. I just got out of bed too fast, is all."

As though she hadn't just made the flimsiest excuse, he said, "You have a doctor's appointment this morning. Get dressed and we'll be off."

She perched on the edge of the bed. "I told you. I'm fine."

"Actually, you got to *I'm* and then you rushed out of the room. So I don't believe you're fine. I think you need to see a doctor, because this could be something serious."

She shook her head. "You're making too much of this."

"And you're not making enough of it."

She crossed her arms and stared at him. "I can't go."

He pressed his hands to his waist. He could be just as stubborn as her. "Why not?"

She didn't speak at first. When she did, her voice was soft, as though the admission was hard for her. "Because bad things always happen to my family when it comes to doctors and hospitals." She shook her head as though chasing away bad memories. Softly but firmly she said, "I can't."

His arms lowered. "I had no idea." He sat beside her. "What happened?"

She glanced away, keeping him from seeing into her expressive eyes. "It started when I was eight." Her voice was rough with emotion. "My mother was walking home from her baking job at the local grocery store. A car came out of nowhere." Pepper drew in a deep breath. "It hit her, sending her tumbling over the roof—" Her voice caught. "The driver kept going. My mother...she was taken to the hospital. I—I remember being allowed to see her before surgery. Her hand was so cold. Her face was a pasty white..." Pepper shook her head as though chasing away the painful images. "She died in surgery."

He reached out to her, hesitated and withdrew his hand. "I'm sorry."

"My grandmother took me in. And then one day she went from being healthy and bossy to being a victim of breast cancer. She went through months of chemo before the doctors declared nothing more could be done." Pepper turned to him. "So you see why I keep my distance from doctors."

"But this is different. You'll be fine."

"Exactly." She stood. "That's why I don't need to go."

He got to his feet. His gaze met hers. They stood there staring at each other for the longest time.

He sighed. "Has anyone told you that you're particularly stubborn?"

"I believe my mother had mentioned it on occasion. So, are you going to stand there all day?"

He rubbed the back of his neck. How was he going to get through to her that she really needed a doctor to examine her?

As though in answer to his thoughts, her face grew pale. She pressed a hand to her stomach before rushing out of the room once more. His concern for her health intensified.

When she returned a little bit later, she was

still pale. "Well, don't just stand there. I have to get ready."

At last he was making progress. "Don't take long. I had to call in a favor to get this appointment."

"I won't. I have work to do. And so do you."

He was already reaching for his phone again as he headed for the door. Once the bedroom door was closed, he started texting his assistant. He told her to cancel any meetings that didn't have to do with the new store launch. And then he had her push back his remaining meetings.

She asked him if anything was wrong. It wasn't like him not to come into the office first thing in the morning, much less cancel important meetings. He assured her that everything was fine. At least, he hoped so.

He was making a big deal of nothing.

And that's exactly what Pepper told the doctor a short time later. The man was older, with silver hair and observant eyes behind his gold-rimmed glasses. He was a quiet man who only spoke when he needed to, but he appeared to listen to everything Pepper nervously said.

It wasn't that she was worried there was something wrong with her. She knew it was just stress—lots of stress. Who wouldn't feel the pressure in her situation? And that's exactly what she told the doctor.

"So you see," she told the doctor. "I'm just stressed out. Simon is worrying about nothing. If you could just tell him that, we can get out of your way."

"We'll just wait for your test results. It won't be much longer."

Simon was out in the waiting room. She could just imagine him pacing a hole in the carpet. Who'd have guessed Simon was such a worrier?

The doctor started for the door.

"Could you have someone show Simon back here?" she asked.

The doctor nodded in his quiet way.

Besides, it would help to have someone distract her. Otherwise, she would soon be climbing the walls, wanting to get out of here. Her grandmother had come to the doctor for one thing and walked out with orders to have tests done for something else entirely.

Was that what was going to happen to her? Surely not. She was just letting her imagination get the best of her. It was this place. It gave her the creeps...

The door opened and Simon poked his head inside. "The nurse said I could come back."

Pepper sat on the edge of the paper-lined examination table. Her legs dangled over the edge. "I'm almost ready to go."

Simon stepped into the room and closed the door. "Everything okay?"

She nodded. "I told you. It's just stress."

He let out a sigh. "That's good. You had me worried."

"You should have listened to me."

"So what are we waiting for?"

"Your doctor. He's the kind that likes to dot all his i's and cross his t's. I noticed he even has all his charts on paper still."

"He's older. He's set in his ways. But don't worry, he knows what he's doing."

She nodded in understanding. "He just has a couple of tests that he's waiting on."

Simon rested his hands on his waist as he rocked from side to side. He looked about as comfortable as she did. They both just needed a distraction.

"What would you be doing if you were at work today?"

He glanced up with a surprised look. "You're interested in my work?"

She shrugged. "Sure. Why not?"

He sighed. "I'd be working on the new chain of stores we're prepared to open in the coming year."

"That sounds so exciting. I'll just be happy to reopen the bakery by Valentine's Day, if I'm really lucky."

"Don't worry. I'm sure you'll be up and running in no time."

If only he was right. But she didn't want to talk about the bakery. Not right now.

She noticed he wasn't smiling. In fact, he'd frowned when he mentioned the new stores.

"What's bothering you about the new stores?"

He glanced at her. "Why do you think something is wrong?"

"Just a feeling I get. Talk to me. Sometimes it helps to vocalize your concerns." So long as the topic wasn't about those test results.

"Because there's nothing to make the chain stand out."

"Won't you have Ross Toys designed for pets?"

"Yes."

"Well, there you go. Ross Toys is world renowned. Pet owners will want only the best for their four-legged babies."

"Agreed. But I feel that we're missing something. I just can't put my finger on it. But I'll know it when I see it."

"Wish I could be of more help—"

Tap. Tap.

The door opened and the doctor stepped inside. The moment of truth had arrived. And Pepper was pretty certain the doctor was going to confirm her self-diagnosis of too much stress.

In fact, she was so certain that she said, "There's nothing wrong with me, right?"

The doctor smiled and gazed at her from behind his bifocals. "Not exactly."

"What is it?" Simon asked. "And when is she going to get better?"

"I'd say in seven or so months."

"What?" Simon asked.

Realization was dawning on Pepper. She'd been so stressed over the bakery and the messy breakup with Simon, not to mention the paparazzi, that she'd missed what was right in front of her face. All the pieces fell into place.

"You're pregnant," the doctor said.

He continued to talk and handed her information, but all she could think about was that she was pregnant with Simon Ross's baby. When she finally gathered her wits, she glanced at Simon.

He looked like his whole world had just blown up. She supposed in a way it had.

As with the fire, she had no idea how to deal with this latest surprise.

CHAPTER EIGHT

COULD THIS REALLY be happening?

He was going to be a father?

No words were spoken on the ride home, but it was a far from quiet ride. Rapid chaotic thoughts ricocheted in Simon's mind. Pregnant? They were pregnant? He was going to be a father?

How could this be? Well, he knew exactly how it had happened. In fact, he could replay the night of conception scene by vivid scene in his mind. And that's how he knew it was possible.

And here he touted himself as such a cautious man. A man who planned for things and didn't take unnecessary risks. Long ago, he'd sworn to himself that he was never going to have kids. He couldn't take a chance that he would mess them up as badly as his father had with him.

And what had he done? Broken that promise to himself.

He didn't even remember the elevator ride from the underground garage up to the penthouse. He unlocked the front door and stepped aside to allow Pepper to enter.

"Pepper?" When she turned to him with a stunned look still in her eyes, he said, "We need to talk."

She nodded before heading into the living room. She perched on the edge of the couch for a few seconds. Then she stood and moved to the window. She didn't say anything, leaving it up to him to start this difficult conversation.

"Did you know?" He wanted to think she hadn't purposely been keeping him in the dark, but he had to know for sure.

"Is that what you think? That I was keeping this great big secret from you?"

"You kept refusing to go to the doctor. If you already knew you were pregnant that would explain it."

"No." Her voice was adamant. "I didn't know until the doctor told both of us. If I was trying to keep it a secret, do you think I would have asked you back to the exam room?"

She did have a good point. But he wasn't ready to accept that he was going to be a father. Not yet. "And the baby... You're positive it's mine?"

Her gaze narrowed into a glare. "Unlike you,

I don't immediately jump from one relationship to the next."

He supposed he might deserve that comment. Until now, he'd never had a reason to remain in a relationship. But everything was changing rapidly and he was struggling to keep up.

He raked his fingers through his hair, not caring what it looked like. "What are we going to do?"

"We? When did you and I become a *we*?"

"When your pregnancy test came up positive."

She crossed her arms. "I can do this myself."

He restrained a sigh of relief. On the ride home, he'd thought about their circumstances and he'd come to one conclusion. He was not under any circumstances following in his family's misguided steps and getting married out of some misguided sense of obligation.

His mother had been pregnant with him when she'd married his father. It had been the single biggest mistake of both their lives—at least that's the way he saw it. His mother might have a different opinion. But no matter what, a baby would not change his stance on marriage—it wasn't for him.

"You don't have to do it alone," he said. "But I'm not getting married."

"Neither am I. Not a chance."

He had to admit that he was shocked at her adamant response. "I didn't know you were opposed to marriage. Or is it me that you object to?"

"Why does it matter? It's not like you're offering."

It was true. He shouldn't care. He took off his suit coat and tossed it over the back of the couch. He paced back and forth. This bickering wasn't getting them anywhere. They had to make a plan.

He may not be into marriage, but that didn't mean he was walking away from his obligation. He definitely wouldn't do that. He wasn't sure he was father material. In fact, he was quite certain he was a less-than-ideal candidate. But he could and would support both Pepper and the baby. It was more than his father ever did for him and his mother.

The memories came flooding back. His father was a man with two faces. The smiling, charming man for friends and acquaintances. But behind closed doors, his father was a totally different man. Nothing was ever good enough for him. And if something was wrong, it was always Simon's mother's fault.

Simon squeezed his eyes closed, blocking out the painful images. But there was one thing he couldn't escape—his fear that lurking within him were the same traits his father had. What if he ended up hurting Pepper and, indirectly, their child? Not physically. He'd never ever raise a hand to a woman or a child. But emotionally, he had scars that he couldn't move beyond.

His blood ran cold. That couldn't happen.

He didn't know what to do about his DNA. There was no way to run from it—to hide from the genes that made him. And then there were the things he'd seen and heard growing up. The yelling, the fighting—it was all he'd known. Could a person really change what had been practically stamped upon his DNA? He highly doubted it.

The key to his child having a happy, loving home was Pepper. She was so full of goodness that it radiated from her. She loved life. She loved baking. She loved tending to her customers—including him.

He'd never forget the morning when he'd gotten word that his childhood friend had unexpectedly died. He'd felt lower than low because he'd let distance grow in the relationship. His friend, Clay, had tried over the years to rekindle the relationship, but Simon had let his drive for business and his need to become someone totally different from his father be his sole focus. That gray drizzly morning, after hearing of his friend's unexpected death, he'd strolled into the Polka Dotted Bakery. He'd been out walking aimlessly, as sleep had evaded him.

And there had been Pepper. She'd been like a ray of sunshine in a dark, stormy sky. And he'd clung to that bright light. She'd never known how much her company had meant to him.

Instead, they'd just sat there talking about the bakery and a bunch of trivial things. And yet that conversation was what he'd needed to survive his guilt—to keep putting one foot in front of the other as he'd attended the funeral, as he'd faced his own mortality.

And then the next week, when he just couldn't stay away, he'd made his way back to the bakery. He didn't know if she'd be there. At the time, he didn't know that she owned the bakery. Still, he'd had to go back if there was a chance that he'd see her again—talk to her again.

If she could do that for a perfect stranger— make that much of a positive impact—he was quite certain she would make the perfect mother for his son or daughter.

* * *

Pepper turned her back to Simon.

He wasn't the only one caught off guard by this news.

A baby changed everything. It meant opening her heart to another person for the first time in a long time. The thought stilled the breath in her lungs.

She wasn't ready for this. She'd lost so much already. The thought of caring for someone else, a little human counting on her for everything, was daunting. But the baby didn't have a choice in these matters.

And neither did she. Pepper moved her hand over her abdomen, imagining the little baby inside her. She loved it already. How could she not?

With a baby to support, she'd need the bakery. If only the fire marshal would complete his report so she could get the repairs started.

She glanced over her shoulder at Simon as he yanked his tie loose and unbuttoned the collar of his white dress shirt. For a man known for his coolness in some of the toughest business negotiations, he had certainly lost his cool when he'd found out he was going to be a father.

But she had to wonder if he was planning to be

in the baby's life. After all, a baby wouldn't actually fit into his glass-and-modern-art decor. But could he really turn his back on his own child?

She sensed Simon stopping behind her. She turned to him and their gazes met. They couldn't leave things like this. She had to know if she was in this all alone.

He cleared his throat. "I'm sorry I'm not handling this better. I never thought I'd be in this position."

"I know you don't want to get married. And neither do I. But I need to know if you're planning to be in our child's life?"

"I'll pay child support."

"What about partial custody or visitation?"

He didn't say anything.

Pepper went on, because she had strong feelings about the subject. "I know fatherhood might not have been something you planned for your future, but now that it's a reality, I hope you'll be a part of the baby's life."

His troubled gaze met hers. "You don't know what you're asking."

"I do know. I grew up never knowing my father. I always thought someday my mother would tell me about him. But then she was killed and my chance to learn about him died with her. I don't want our child to wonder about you."

His gaze searched hers. "You want me to be a regular part of the child's life?"

She nodded. "It's important not only for our child, but for you too. I know you, Simon. You'd never forgive yourself if you weren't a part of our son or daughter's life."

He shook his head. "There's so much you don't know about me." He glanced away. "I'm not this great guy you think I am. I have skeletons in my closet."

"Everyone does. It's what you do about them that decides what sort of person you are."

His gaze returned to hers. "You do know that you'll never have to worry about money. I'll make sure the baby has everything they could possibly want—"

"Except you?"

He shrugged. "I… I don't know. I need to think."

It wasn't a yes, but it wasn't a no either. So she'd take it.

"We were both caught off guard today," she said. "It'll take time to figure this out. But I hope you'll keep an open mind where the baby is concerned."

He nodded. "I will."

"You should probably go to the office and deal with the upcoming store opening. I have a party to finish preparing for." And then, realizing that the news of the baby might have changed their arrangement, she asked, "Is it all right if I still use the kitchen?"

His eyes widened with surprise. "Of course. You'll be here when I get home?"

"I will."

He left for the office looking a bit disheveled compared to his normal clean-cut appearance. She couldn't blame him. It had been quite a day and it wasn't even lunchtime yet.

Where did they go from here?

CHAPTER NINE

HE'D THOUGHT AND thought and then thought some more.

The answers about the baby still eluded him.

How was he going to be a good father when he'd never had one?

The next morning, Simon sleepwalked through his usual routine. He'd been up most of the night tossing and turning. His thoughts halted as he opened his bedroom door. He inhaled the most delicious aroma. He followed it to the kitchen, where he heard Christmas carols playing and the sweet sound of Pepper's voice.

He placed his hand on the swinging door and pushed. He entered the kitchen to find Pepper in a black apron, pulling a tray out of the oven. She turned and placed it on the enormous island. Her gaze strayed across him and she pressed her lips together, silencing her beautiful voice. She didn't smile, but she didn't frown either. That was something at least.

She moved to her phone and silenced the music. "Sorry. I didn't mean to bother you. Sometimes I get to baking and totally forget about everything else."

"It's not a problem. In fact, I like hearing you sing. You have a beautiful voice." He didn't come in here to flatter her, but he'd been moved by her voice. "Are you feeling better this morning?"

She shrugged. "It comes and goes."

He glanced around at all the finished baked goods. "You must have been up for hours."

"I didn't sleep well."

"Me either." He walked over to take a closer look at the gingerbread men on the kitchen island. "I'm glad to see you're making yourself at home."

She arched a brow at him. "Are you?"

She doubted him? But then again, he hadn't been the most congenial host after they got the news about the baby. "I wasn't myself yesterday."

Pepper placed another tray of cupcakes in the oven and set the timer. Then she turned back to him. "I want you to know that this pregnancy wasn't planned."

"I didn't think it was."

Pepper was the most honest person he'd ever

known. And whether he wanted to admit it or not, she was good for him. She made him want to be a better person—to know that if he kept trying, he could overcome whatever stood before him. And his life was noticeably dimmer without her in it.

Her gaze met his. "Do you mean that?"

He nodded. "I do. And I'd like you to stay here, until your apartment is repaired."

She shook her head. "I don't think that's a good idea."

"You're better off here than in some motel. If you need anything, I'll be here for you." This was more important to him than he'd ever imagined. "And you can use the kitchen to continue doing as much of your work as you feel up to."

Before she could say anything, the doorbell rang.

A frown pulled at his face. He wasn't expecting anyone. He rarely entertained guests in his penthouse. He preferred to keep it as his private domain.

"I'll be right back." He turned for the door.

With a doorman, unannounced guests were limited to those who were preapproved. The list was quite short. But it could be a delivery for Pepper.

He swung the door open and found his mother standing there, every dark strand of her pixie cut in place and her makeup perfectly done. She did not look like a woman on the verge of her six-tieth birthday.

"Mother, what are you doing here?" He didn't know whether to be more shocked that she was at his place or that she'd arrived at such an early hour.

She swept past him into the foyer. "Is it true?"

"Is what true?" As he closed the door, he re-alized he had absolutely no idea what she was talking about.

Her eyes widened. "You haven't heard the news?"

"Obviously not." He worried that something had gone terribly wrong with his new expansion. He knew his competitors were not happy about the launch, but he'd been able to overcome every roadblock they'd thrown in his way.

His mother pulled out her phone and quickly pulled up an article. He was curious to see what had her so worked up that she'd left home be-fore the time she normally had her second cup of coffee. She held her phone out to him.

He took it from her and stared at the photo. It

was of him and Pepper leaving the doctor's office. His gut twisted in an uncomfortable knot.

Billionaire Bachelor to Billionaire Daddy!

An unnamed source said the happy couple had reunited and were now expecting their first child. His hand tightened around the phone. A frustrated growl grew deep in his throat. There was more to the story, but his anger kept him from comprehending the rest of the article. This couldn't be happening.

The last time the paparazzi got involved, Pepper had ended things with him. The thing he didn't know was how big of a part the press had played in her decision. If the paparazzi had left them alone, would things have gone differently?

"So, is it true? Are you finally making me a grandmother?" There was a hopeful glint in his mother's eyes that surprised him.

"Simon?" Pepper stepped into the foyer and came to a stop upon noticing his mother. "Sorry. I didn't mean to interrupt."

"Is this her?" his mother asked.

Pepper's puzzled gaze moved between him and his mother. He'd been really hoping to avoid this for a while, but it looked like he had no other choice.

"Mother, this is Pepper Kane. Pepper, meet my mother, Sandra."

Pepper stepped forward, shook hands and exchanged pleasantries.

Simon opened the door. "Mother, we'll have to visit later. Pepper and I have some things to discuss."

His mother's eyes lit up as she moved toward the door. "So it's true."

It wasn't a question; it was a statement. And he wasn't in any position to correct her. "We'll talk later."

"Yes, we will." His mother glanced over at Pepper. "It was so nice to meet you, dear."

"Um, nice to meet you too." Pepper looked utterly confused and he couldn't blame her.

His mother gave him a butterfly kiss on the cheek and then left with a trail of Chanel No. 5 in her wake. His mother wasn't born into money, in fact, she was born far from it. Still, when he'd established himself in the business world and was able to care for her, she'd taken to the elevation in her lifestyle like a duck to water. After what his father had put her through for years, Simon was glad she'd found some happiness—even if the uneasiness between them still existed.

He closed the door. He wanted to shield Pepper from the headlines, but he knew the reporters would flock to the building, if they weren't here already. There was no hiding from this story.

"That was nice of your mother to stop by. You should have invited her to stay. I have your coffee started and there are plenty of pastries in the kitchen."

He shook his head. "Now isn't the time for visitors. You and I have something to discuss."

Although coffee did sound good. He made his way to the kitchen and poured himself a cup. He nearly moaned in delight when he took his first sip.

His gaze moved to Pepper. "It tastes just like the coffee at the bakery."

She smiled and nodded. "I take it you like it."

"I love it."

"Drink as much as you want. Now that I'm pregnant, I can't have it."

He hadn't thought of that. There were a lot of things he hadn't thought of yet. And he didn't want to ruin this easy moment between them. But it was better she heard it from him than to be blindsided by the paparazzi.

"My mother stopped by for a reason."

"Is something wrong?"

"In a way." How did he tell her this gently? He didn't think there was any way to do it. "She knows about the baby."

"What? But how? I didn't think we were to the point of telling people."

"We aren't. I—I didn't," he stammered. "I wouldn't do that without talking to you first. She read it online."

"What?" Pepper's voice rose.

"Apparently, someone inside the doctor's office spotted us and sold the story. I don't know if it was staff, which I highly doubt, or if it was another patient."

Pepper worried her bottom lip as though she was replaying the events. "There were a few people around when the nurse rushed into the waiting room to give me the prenatal vitamins that I'd forgotten in the exam room." She looked crestfallen. "This is all my fault. If I hadn't forgotten them—"

"It's not your fault." He stepped up to her and gazed deep into her eyes. "None of this is your fault."

She pressed a hand to her abdomen. "I can't do this."

Worry gripped him. "Do what?"

She moved her hand between the two of them. "This. Everything you do is headline news. I don't want our baby caught up in a media frenzy—"

"Don't worry. We'll work things out."

Her eyes filled with fear. "You can't promise me that."

He sighed. "You're right. I can't promise the media will leave us alone, but there has to be a way to minimize their interference. We have a lot to figure out." And then before he analyzed the right and wrong of it, he pulled her into his arms, attempting to will away her inner turmoil.

He wanted to make this better for her, but the problem with success was that everything you did made headlines.

He continued to hold her close. "Together, we'll do what is best for the baby."

CHAPTER TEN

AND SO SHE'D STAYED.

Pepper hadn't been sure in the beginning of their living arrangement if it was a good idea. But with the paparazzi hunting for a story, she didn't have much choice. Trying to stay in a motel with the press hounding her would have been a disaster. At least when she was in Simon's penthouse, they couldn't photograph her.

And she was able to leave through the garage in a private car with tinted windows that Simon had put at her disposal. She didn't like having to rely on him, but with the baby's safety to take into consideration, she'd decided to take him up on his offer.

But one day had turned into two days. And two days had turned into a week. At last, the paparazzi had moved on to a new scandal. Pepper felt sorry for the young woman at the center of it. She knew what it was to be hounded day and night.

Friday afternoon, she had no baking scheduled. It wasn't her day at the shelter. And she had no idea what to do with all the time on her hands.

With Simon going out of his way for her, she wanted to repay him. It had to be more than his morning coffee and daily supply of cherry turnovers. She wanted to do more. But what? She frowned as her mind drew a blank.

Her gaze moved around the stark, monochrome penthouse. Pepper sighed. This place exuded money, but it was so cold. Not temperature-wise, as she had the fireplace lit, but in a personal way. She noticed there weren't any photos, not of him, not of his family, not of anyone. She found that strange.

She would be lost without her photos. Her heart clutched. What if they'd been lost in the fire?

Immediately, tears pricked the back of her eyes. She told herself to calm down. Though they hadn't let her into the apartment yet, they'd said the damage on the second floor was limited to water and smoke. She just had to hope the pictures had survived.

Instead of sitting around worrying, she knew she had to get busy. Her grandmother used to say that idle hands were the devil's workshop. In Pepper's case, it was an idle mind.

If she was going to continue to stay here, something had to be done with the place. There wasn't one thing around the penthouse that resembled Christmas. Not even a red or green anything. The color scheme was limited to black, white and gray.

The penthouse exuded a high-powered executive lifestyle. But it didn't look like anyone actually lived there. She turned in a circle, taking in the two long couches forming a right angle near the black marble fireplace. A large smoked-glass coffee table was devoid of everything, not even a houseplant or magazine was on it. How did this man live like this?

And then she realized the answer: he lived at his office. If it wasn't for her presence, he wouldn't be home nearly as much. Maybe she needed to give him a reason to come home—a place to unwind. Since the Polka Dotted Bakery, where he used to let down his guard, was currently out of commission, she'd have to create a homey atmosphere here. Or as close to it as she could get.

She grabbed her purse, coat and knit cap. Out the door she went. She was a lady on a mission.

* * *

What in the world…?

Simon came to a stop at the edge of the living room.

He blinked, making sure he wasn't seeing things. He hadn't been sleeping well, with all the latest developments in his life and a big launch ahead of him. He blinked again—but there was still a ginormous pine tree leaning against the wall. What in the world?

How did it get in here?

He glanced around for Pepper. It was too big for her to carry, but he'd bet his business that she had something to do with its presence.

"Pepper!"

He wasn't a man who normally raised his voice, but these obviously weren't normal times. And all he'd wanted to do was come home, yank off his tie, undo the top buttons on his dress shirt, have a drink and unwind.

"Pepper!"

"Why are you yelling?" The voice came from behind him.

He spun around to find Pepper standing in the doorway with shopping bags in her hands. He rushed forward and took the bags from her so she could take off her coat and hat.

He returned to the living room and his gaze settled on the Christmas tree—the source of his agitation. He set the bags on the couch and turned to her. "What is this doing here?"

She pulled off her cap and smoothed her hands down over her hair. When her gaze landed on the tree, a big smile lit up her pretty face. Instantly, his agitation started to fade.

"It looks perfect in here. I was afraid it would be too small, but I also worried about getting something too big, you know, with the elevator and everything."

He didn't do holidays. The only ones he endured were those for employees or business acquaintances. But he certainly didn't have a tree and decorations for his own benefit.

"It has to go." His tone was firm. His mind was made up.

"What?" Pepper's eyes widened in astonishment. "But why?"

"I don't want it here." He rubbed the back of his neck. He shouldn't be so brusque with her. It wasn't like he'd told her about his "no Christmas" policy. "I don't celebrate Christmas."

"You don't believe in Santa?"

There was such sincerity and awe in her voice that for a minute, he thought she was being serious. When his gaze caught hers, he couldn't read her thoughts. "Please don't tell me you believe in Santa."

She shrugged. "I don't believe there's a man who lives at the North Pole who delivers Christmas presents around the world in one night, but I believe in the spirit of Christmas. I believe it lives in each of us."

He shook his head. "Not me."

She frowned at him. "Even you."

He shook his head again. "There's nothing good about Christmas."

Her mouth gaped open. "How can you say that?"

"Because Christmas was always the worst time in our house." It didn't bring their family together. Instead the holiday drove a bigger wedge between him, his mother and his father.

"Really?" Sympathy shone clearly in her big green eyes. "I'm sorry."

He shrugged off her sympathy. He didn't want her to feel sorry for him. He just wanted her to make this Christmas tree go away.

He went to sit on the couch and bumped into her packages, which spilled onto the floor. There were all sorts of Christmas decorations—things for trimming the tree. He inwardly groaned.

He knelt down and began stuffing the shiny red balls back in the bag. The next thing he knew, Pepper was kneeling beside him. Together, they worked to clean up the mess of decorations.

As the time went by, the shock of finding a Christmas tree in his place wore off and he realized Pepper could never understand the horrific memories he had attached to the holiday. He was quite certain they were much different than her experience with the holiday.

Simon settled on the floor and leaned back against the couch. He needed to smooth things over with Pepper. They'd come a long way this week toward being friendly with each other again and he didn't want to ruin their progress. "I'm sorry for grouching at you. I was caught off guard when I came through the door and found a tree in the living room."

"I understand. I should have asked you first. I… I wanted to surprise you. Obviously, I did that, but not in a good way like I'd been hoping."

He sighed. "I'm not like other people."

He was broken. But he couldn't admit that to Pepper. He couldn't have her look at him like he was less of a man. Or worse, with sympathy in her eyes. He'd spent his whole life proving he was no longer that scared, helpless child.

"You're definitely unlike anyone I've ever known." She sent him a hesitant smile. "Have you noticed this amazing Manhattan penthouse you live in? Most people could only imagine living in a place like this."

"It wasn't always that way. I didn't grow up with a silver spoon in my mouth." He was very proud of the empire he'd built, one toy, one store, at a time.

"What was Christmas like when you were young?"

This was not the direction he wanted the conversation to go. "It was fine."

"Fine? That's an odd description." Pepper placed the bag on the floor and then sat on the couch near him. "We never had much when I was little, but my mother made the most of the holiday. We went caroling and sledding. We baked cookies and watched Christmas movies. She emphasized the time we spent together instead of the lack of presents under the tree."

"Your mother sounds like she was great."

"She was, but…"

He moved so he could look at her. "But what?"

"She was eccentric and definitely flamboyant. That's hard to deal with as a kid, when all you want in the world is to fit in and be just like everyone else." Pepper pulled a strand of lights out of another bag. "I bet you had the perfect Christmases—the kind in those holiday movies."

"Far from it. My mother tried to have a fun Christmas, but my father always ruined it. He would be furious and accuse her of wasting money—money that belonged to him." He could still hear the echo of his father's booming voice. Every word he bellowed was laced with anger. "My Christmases were more *Die Hard* than *National Lampoon's Christmas Vacation.*"

"I'm sorry. I never imagined."

"Most people don't. It's the way I like to keep it."

"Is that why your place is so…so impersonal?"

It didn't surprise him that she didn't care for his ultramodern, minimalist style. It was the complete opposite of her warm, cozy bakery. "It's not to your liking?"

She glanced away. "It…it just needs some personality."

He glanced around the room, trying to see it through Pepper's eyes. Whereas Pepper's bakery had photos on the walls, his penthouse only had a large skyline photo of the city at night. At the bakery, there were knickknacks, including a stuffed dog that he'd meant to ask her about but never had the chance. He didn't have knick-knacks. He'd never even thought of getting any.

The Polka Dotted Bakery oozed charm and hominess that made it unique. His penthouse was cool and detached. He realized that if he were to pack up his clothes, he could move out and it would be ready for the next occupant. It was more a hotel room than home.

Simon was stunned. He'd never seen his penthouse like this before. It was quite eye-opening. And not in a good way.

"Don't worry," Pepper said. "I'll have the tree taken away."

He shook his head. What would it hurt to let her keep it? After all, it must be important to her or she wouldn't have gone to the trouble of buying it or the decorations. When she moved back to her apartment, he'd have it delivered to her.

"The tree—it can stay."

Pepper's eyes lit up. "Are you sure? I mean, you didn't seem all that happy it was here."

"Are you trying to talk me out of this?"

"No. No. I just wanted to make sure you're truly okay with it. After all, this is your place."

"And for the moment, it's yours too." He didn't know why he'd said that. Maybe he just wanted her to feel at home. Because he certainly didn't mean to imply that this situation would be anything other than temporary.

He got to his feet and turned to head to his study. He had some work to do. In fact, he had a lot of it to do. Normally, he'd have stayed at the office until late, trying to catch up, which never happened. But knowing Pepper was here had lured him home. He told himself it was the right thing to do, as he was the host and she was his guest. But deep down, he knew it was more than that. He just wasn't ready to admit it to himself.

"Simon?"

He paused at the entrance to the hallway and turned around. "Did you need something?"

"Yes. You."

"Me?"

She nodded. "Don't you want to help?"

"Help?"

She gave him a funny look. "With trimming the tree?"

"No."

Her beautiful face morphed into a frown. "Oh."

She turned away and began rifling through the bags on the couch. He'd hurt her feelings.

He hadn't meant to. The fact of the matter was that outside of the office, he kept to himself as much as possible. Sure, he had the occasional obligatory dates to social functions, but he never invited those dates back here—back to his domain.

Pepper was the first woman in his penthouse. And he had to admit that his interaction with her was a lot different than dealing with his employees at the office.

At the office, he told people what to do and they did it. They didn't ask for his company. They didn't want to have personal conversations. They all had one goal—to make Ross Toys the biggest and the best.

But here with Pepper, he'd lost his footing. He couldn't boss her around. He subdued a laugh at the thought. If he did try telling Pepper what to do, she'd probably knock some sense into him with her rolling pin.

And yet they did have a common goal—their baby. If they were going to raise a normal, well-adjusted child, they were going to have to learn to make compromises. Lots of them. He supposed this was one of those compromises.

And though it went against every grain in his body, he returned to the couch. He suppressed the memories of his past and the horrid Christmases that his family had shared. He would do it for Pepper and the baby.

"How can I help?" he asked.

She shook her head, not looking at him. "It's fine. I've got this. I'm sure you have more important things to do."

"This is important to you, so it's important to me."

That got her attention. She turned to him. Her green gaze studied him. "Why?"

"Why what? Why am I helping?" When she nodded, he said, "Honestly, because you want me to."

"Why do you still hate Christmas after all these years?"

Her question poked at him in the most sensitive spot. He didn't talk about his past with anyone, including his own mother—especially his mother. If it were up to him, he'd just as soon forget about the past—about Christmas, about family.

But Pepper and soon the baby weren't going to make that possible. Instead, he would have to figure out a way to deal with it. He just wasn't sure how to do that except to push through and do what needed to be done as quickly as possible.

He reached for a box of ornaments. "Shall I put these on the tree?"

"You aren't going to answer my question?"

"It doesn't matter." It did matter. It mattered a lot.

But he didn't want to scare Pepper away for good. And so he kept quiet about the other skeletons in his closet. It was just the way it needed to be.

CHAPTER ELEVEN

Talk about your mysteries.

Simon Ross was one walking puzzle.

And Pepper wanted so badly to sort out the pieces that made him whole. But she had to be careful how hard she pushed him for answers. Or he'd totally shut down on her.

Pepper picked up the string of twinkle lights. They were assorted colors. She loved colors. It was a part of her mother that had rubbed off on her. The older she got, the less she cared about what people thought of her and just let herself enjoy her differences.

Except Simon.

She did care what he thought of her. She knew she shouldn't, but she couldn't help herself. It wasn't that she was going to change herself to suit him, but now that they were living together, she hoped he'd continue to accept her with her sometimes out-of-control hair and her eccentric tendencies. Perhaps she was more like her mother than she'd ever considered.

"Something on your mind?" Simon's voice drew her from her thoughts.

"Ah, yes. I was wondering if I got enough lights." Her gaze moved to the two bundles of lights and then moved to the tree. "The tree looks a lot bigger than I remembered."

His gaze moved to the bundles of lights. "Did you get those from your apartment?"

"Um, no. They still haven't let me inside."

The truth was she'd purchased them from a thrift store. It was where she made a lot of purchases. Paying for the bakery took most of her income. What was left, she had to budget carefully. Still, she just couldn't imagine telling this man, who could afford to buy anything his heart desired, that she was decorating his place with secondhand decorations.

"Let's see about getting the lights on the tree." And just like that he let the subject of the lights' origins drop. Either he knew or it wasn't important to him. Either way, she was relieved.

And so they worked together for the next couple of hours placing the decorations on the tree. She'd greatly underestimated its size. The decorations were sparse. She felt terrible.

Ding, dong.

"I'll get that," Simon said. "It's about time the pizza got here."

Pepper continued to study the tree, trying to figure out how to improve it. If it were in her apartment, she wouldn't have bought one nearly so large, because her ceilings weren't nearly as high. And the decorations wouldn't look so sparse. But here in the luxury penthouse, it looked all wrong.

She moved to the tree and started taking off the ornaments. What had she been thinking? People like Simon, they hired people to decorate their trees with the finest decorations that probably cost more than her annual salary.

"I hope you're hungry…" Simon's words faded away as he spotted her dismantling the decorations. He set the pizza box on the coffee table and moved next to her. "Hey, what are you doing? Rearranging the ornaments? I wasn't sure where to put them."

"I'm taking it down."

"Down?"

She nodded. Her emotions were rising. She remembered what it was like back in school when she'd tried to fit in with the other girls. Her mother had found her some stylish clothes at the thrift store. In the end, it turned out they had been donated by one of the rich girls. The blouse had tiny initials on the cuff—the girl's initials. Pepper had never been so devastated.

This was another of those moments when she was trying to fit in. And there was absolutely nothing she could do to fit into Simon's world. He might as well live on Mars, that's how far apart their realities were.

Her fingers trembled as emotions both new and old coursed through her. Simon placed a hand over hers, stopping her from removing yet another ornament.

"Pepper, talk to me. What's wrong? I know I was hesitant about the tree in the beginning, but I thought we had a good time decorating it."

She concentrated her gaze on his long fingers draped over hers. "I shouldn't have done this. I shouldn't have forced this tree on you. You don't want it."

He clasped his hand with hers. She relaxed her hand within his. It felt natural for them to be holding hands. When did that happen?

His fingers tightened as he led her to the couch. She didn't want to sit down. She knew he was going to want to talk things out, and then she was going to appear even sillier than she already felt.

"Pepper." He paused as though waiting for her to look at him.

She didn't want to face him. The heat of embarrassment was already lapping at her cheeks. Still, she wasn't a wimp. Even when the other kids had made fun of her, she'd stood her ground. As badly as their words had hurt, she'd stood there and faced them down. Why should she do any different now?

And so with all the willpower she could muster, she turned her head until her gaze met Simon's. "We don't need to talk about this. I'll just get rid of the tree and things can go back to the way they were."

"What if that's not what I want?"

"What?" Surely she hadn't heard him correctly. "You can't mean you want the tree."

"Actually, I think I do."

He did? Wait. She was missing something.

"Just a few hours ago, you were telling me it had to go. Now you're telling me it has to stay?" Her gaze searched his as she tried to figure out his abrupt change of mind. "Simon, what's going on?"

He shrugged. "I don't know. Maybe I've been

holding on to my resentment of the past for too long."

"You resented Christmas?" Who resents Christmas? It's the best time of the year.

He rubbed the back of his neck. "What can I say? I'm unusual." His gaze turned back to the tree. "So what do you say? Can we keep the tree?"

She didn't know when this had all gotten so turned around, but somewhere along the way their roles had gotten mixed up. She followed his gaze to the tree. Maybe it wasn't so bad, after all.

"I suppose I could get some more ornaments for it," she said.

"You know, I just might be able to help you with that."

"What? How?"

He headed out of the living room. She followed, having no idea what he was up to now. He headed down the hallway. He stopped outside a closed door. He opened it and flipped on the light.

She glanced inside, finding stacks of cardboard boxes. "What is all of this?"

"Things that were given to me—mostly by my mother. I didn't know what to do with all of the stuff so I put it in here to deal with later." He started opening boxes. "When I first moved in, I remember her bringing over Christmas decorations."

"Did you ever use them?"

"No."

Pepper nodded, though she didn't quite understand. "Can I help you?"

"If you want."

Together, they went through the boxes until they uncovered two boxes of assorted ornaments. They carried them to the living room, where Pepper turned on some Christmas carols.

The longer they worked, the more he loosened up. The more he let down his guard, the more she remembered what drew her to him in the beginning—his deep, warm laughter that filled her with joy, his big smile that filled her with warmth—

"Pepper?" His voice startled her from her thoughts.

She lifted her gaze to meet his. "What did you say?"

He smiled, sending her heart tumbling in her chest. "Something on your mind?"

"No." Heat rushed to her cheeks. Did he know where her thoughts had strayed? Of course not. "What do you need?"

"Some more silver balls. I think I saw some in the box. Never mind, I'll get them." He climbed off the ladder next to the tree.

"I've got it." Pepper rushed to the box.

There were a lot of decorations in it. It'd be nice to find a place for all of them. After all, this penthouse was huge. Plenty of room to use all the decorations.

She reached in the box, moving items around. She didn't see any silver ornaments. She placed items outside the box as she sorted them.

"Found them," she said gleefully.

"I found something too." He held up a ball of greenery with red berries and a gold bow.

"It's pretty. What is it?"

His eyes twinkled with mischief. He raised his arm, dangling the ball over her head. Suddenly she knew it was a mistletoe kissing ball. Her heart raced.

Her gaze moved to Simon. He wasn't going to...

Simon leaned toward her, pressing a kiss to her lips. His mouth was warm and oh-so-tempting. It was as though time stopped. And she didn't want it to start again.

So many nights she'd dreamed about this moment, longed for this moment. And now it was so hard to believe that it was happening—that Simon's mouth was moving over hers.

Was it wrong to give in to the moment? To let herself savor this moment? Her heart and mind were at odds.

Something that felt this good couldn't possibly be wrong. She leaned into him. Her hands landed on his chest—his very firm, very muscular chest. She stifled a moan as common sense got lost in a haze of desire.

Her mouth moved beneath his. A soft moan of pure pleasure formed at the base of her throat. Simon's tongue delved into her mouth. He tasted sweet, like the peppermint candy he'd enjoyed earlier.

Buzz. Buzz.

The sound of the phone brought her feet back to earth. She pulled away from him and pressed her fingers to her sensitive lips.

She backed away from him. Moving out of his gravitational pull, she felt her common sense start to return. She walked to the big window overlooking the city. The millions of lights sparkled like diamonds.

Simon stepped up behind her. "Pepper, I'm sorry. It seemed like a good idea at the time."

"It's okay." Her insides shivered with a rush of emotions. She wasn't okay. Far from it.

"Pepper—"

Buzz. Buzz.

"You should get that." She turned and moved past him.

She picked up the silver ornaments and moved to the tree. She forced her thoughts to the work before her, because every time she recalled the way his lips had moved seductively over hers, her stomach dipped and her face flamed with heat. She couldn't let him see how he'd gotten to her.

By the time Simon finished his call, she'd placed all of the silver ornaments strategically on the tree. Truth be told, she might have put more thought into their placement than was necessary.

"Pepper?" Simon's voice came from behind her.

Her breath hitched in her throat.

Just pretend like the kiss didn't happen. Because it was a mistake. One not to be repeated.

She turned to him. "Do you need something?"

He approached her and then, as though he realized that wasn't a good idea, he stopped. "I'm sorry about that."

"No problem. I know you're an important businessman."

He shook his head. "I meant the kiss. I shouldn't have done it."

"Don't worry. It's already forgotten."

Liar. Liar.

For a moment, neither spoke. It was as though each of them was trying to find their footing once more.

This whole situation was a lot for them to deal with. They didn't need to complicate matters more than they already were. Her hand moved to her still-flat abdomen. It was best for all of them.

CHAPTER TWELVE

SHE'D MADE IT.

The next morning, Pepper stepped through the doorway of Helping Paw. She glanced at the clock, finding she still had some time before lunch. Not as early as she would like, but considering she was beginning to think she'd have to forgo her impromptu visit, she was pleased.

This day had not started as she'd hoped.

Pepper sighed as she ran a hand over her hair, which was pulled back in a messy ponytail— very messy indeed. The day began with her sleeping in and then being hit with a serious bout of morning sickness. She'd hoped it was just a one- or two-time thing, but it appeared it was going to hit her every morning of her first trimester.

But it'd be worth it in the end. She resisted the urge to place a hand on her still-flat abdomen. With every day that passed, her excitement about the baby was growing.

After telling herself that she was done caring for people because the price was too high, she couldn't imagine not loving this baby. It was such a powerful attachment. And though at times it scared her to think how precarious life could be, her love for the baby trumped her fear.

Life right now was challenging enough with the aftermath of a fire to deal with, a very sexy roommate who was off-limits and a penthouse that seemed to grow smaller with each passing day. She supposed she could have given up on volunteering at the shelter—even temporarily. But she knew the shelter was hard-pressed to find people willing to give up their time to help out. And there were so many animals that needed love and support. She couldn't turn her back on them. Not even if it meant her life wouldn't be quite so hectic.

And then there was Daisy. Pepper looked forward to seeing her as much as possible, even on days when she wasn't scheduled to volunteer. They still hadn't been able to put the pup up for adoption, but shy little Daisy was making progress.

"Hey, is everything okay?" Stephanie gazed at her with a worried look on her face.

Pepper forced a smile, hoping it would alleviate her friend's concern. "Yeah, I'm fine."

"You don't look fine." Stephanie gestured to a stool. "Maybe you should sit down."

Did she really look as bad as she felt? Maybe she should have paused and fixed her makeup before rushing over here. She hadn't even thought of stopping for a second look in the mirror before rushing out the door, and that wasn't like her. Not at all.

"Now that you're expecting, you're going to have to slow down," Stephanie said.

It was no secret that she was pregnant. Every single person she knew had read it all over the internet. Even total strangers who recognized her from her picture would offer their congratulations. But at least the paparazzi wasn't following her every minute of the day.

Pepper sat down on the stool. "I can't stay long. I just wanted to check in on Daisy."

Stephanie's brow rose as she nodded. "You two are becoming quite close."

"She trusts me now. That's a big step. The trick is getting Daisy to trust others. I don't know what was done to her in the past, but it was bad. The poor thing. She just needs lots of time and love."

Buzz. Buzz.

Pepper looked at her friend. "You can go ahead and get that."

"It's not my phone."

It rang again. That's when Pepper realized the sound was coming from her coat pocket. "That's strange. It's not my normal ring tone."

She pulled the phone from her pocket and glanced at the screen. Her name and number were displayed. She was calling herself?

Pressing the phone to her ear, Pepper said, "Hello?"

"Pepper. Oh, good." It was Simon's voice. "We mixed up our phones this morning in the kitchen."

"Oh. Sorry."

"If you can let me know where you are, I'll swing by and we can exchange them. I'm really lost without mine. I didn't realize how much information I store on it."

She didn't want him to have to go out of his way. "I can stop by your office."

"No need. I'm still in the car."

She gave him the address. He promised to be there in a few minutes.

"Did I hear correctly?" Stephanie asked. "Simon is coming here?"

Pepper nodded. She wasn't sure how she felt about having him here at the shelter. She knew it shouldn't be a big deal, but with every day that passed, it was like another part of her life was revealed to him. Soon he would know everything about her.

"I'm going to go visit Daisy while I wait." Pepper got to her feet and moved to the back of the building.

Daisy was isolated from the other adoptable dogs, but wouldn't be for much longer. When the puppy saw her, her tail started to wag. Pepper wanted to believe it was her the dog was excited about and not the little dog biscuits she'd started baking and kept in her pocket.

"Hey, girl. You look happy today." Pepper opened the crate. "Let's go stretch your legs."

Daisy wiggled around excitedly while Pepper tried to attach the leash. "You are a wiggle tail."

The leash attached, Pepper placed Daisy on the floor and off they went, strolling along the back of the building. It was taking Daisy a while to be leash trained, but she was finally taking to it.

"Pepper?" It was Simon's voice.

Daisy stopped in her tracks. And the teeny tiny puppy let out a really big howl. Pepper didn't know such a large sound could come from something so little.

Pepper knelt down and picked Daisy up. She ran a hand over Daisy's short fur. "It's okay, girl." When Daisy continued to howl, Pepper decided to distract her with a biscuit. It worked.

And then to Simon, she said, "We're over here."

When Simon stopped in front of her, his gaze moved from her to Daisy and then back again. "I didn't know you worked here."

"She doesn't." Greta stepped up to Simon and extended her hand, with her long, polished deep red nails. "I run this shelter. And you would be Simon Ross."

He turned a blank expression to the woman. He hesitated for a brief moment before shaking her hand.

"So what brings you here?" Greta's dark eyes glinted with interest.

Pepper stepped forward. "I think he's here for—"

Greta stepped between Pepper and Simon. "I've got this." The woman never took her eyes off Simon. "Pepper, don't you have something to do?"

Pepper gaped at the back of the woman's head.

Had Greta really just dismissed her from speaking to the father of her baby? How dare she?

Just as Pepper was prepared to set Greta straight, Daisy started barking. While Greta was distracted, Simon signaled for her to let this woman dig her own hole.

"Pepper, take that little monster back to her cage."

She was tempted to ask the woman if she was referring to herself. Instead, she quietly walked away.

Had that really happened?

Simon was so relieved to have disentangled himself from Greta. For some reason, he thought people that headed up animal shelters would be kind and generous. Obviously, that wasn't always the case. But since the shelter meant so much to Pepper, he'd minded his manners and not told the woman exactly what he thought of her rude and pushy tactics.

Simon caught up with Pepper and Daisy. "Does that woman really run the shelter?"

Pepper nodded. "No one can figure out how she got the job."

"She certainly doesn't like animals."

"Not at all."

"But she does like money. She hit me up for a very large donation."

Pepper's cheeks grew pink. "I'm so sorry."

"Don't be. I wasn't giving that woman anything." When he realized that might have come out wrong, he added, "But if you were to ask, that would be a totally different matter."

"I might take you up on the offer. The shelter is hurting for money so badly that they're starting to turn away animals." Worry reflected in her eyes. "We've tried everything we can think of to raise money, but it never seems to be enough. But that isn't the reason you're here."

He made a mental note to have the shelter looked into. He was more than willing to make regular donations, but first he wanted to make sure where his money would be going. And he didn't want Greta to take credit for the shelter's turnaround.

"I have your phone." He held out the phone to her, and with her free hand she removed his from her pocket.

"And here's yours."

Daisy started to wiggle, so Pepper put her back on the ground. "Would you like another treat?"

Arff! Arff! Arff!

"I'd swear she knows what the word *treat* means."

Daisy barked again.

Pepper pulled another treat from her pocket. She held the biscuit out to Simon. "Would you like to give it to her?"

He shook his head. "I don't think so. I don't know anything about dogs."

"Well, then you and Daisy will get along fine. She doesn't know much about people, but she's learning." Pepper placed the little biscuit in his hand. "Place it on the flat of your hand and hold it out to her. She'll do the rest."

Simon crouched down and did as Pepper said. Daisy was hesitant, but couldn't resist the treat. He couldn't help but smile at the eager look on the puppy's face or the thumping of her tail. She was really cute—not that he was a dog person.

When he straightened, she said, "Maybe you want to look around and adopt a dog. Or perhaps you're more of a cat person. Or maybe one of each."

He shook his head. "Not me. I'm not good with animals."

"Daisy might disagree. Huh, girl?"

Simon glanced down as the little dog crunched on the biscuit. "She really likes that treat."

"She does. I've been working on perfecting them."

Simon glanced at her. "Perfecting?"

Pepper nodded. "I've started making treats for the dogs. At first I was just playing around, trying something different. But with the shelter hurting for money, they can't afford extras for the animals. So I've been making as many treats as I can and bringing them into the shelter. The dogs seem to really like them."

He paused as a thought came him. "These treats… You've developed your own recipes?"

She nodded. "I figure if I can make cake recipes, it can't be much harder to make pet-friendly recipes."

This was what his Pet Playground stores were missing—the personal touch. They needed something that wasn't mass produced. They needed Pepper's treats. But how would he make it possible to have fresh baked treats in each store of a chain that eventually would extend from coast to coast?

"Simon?" Pepper looked at him with a look of concern.

"Sorry. I just had a thought about work." He thought back to their conversation. "Is there anything you can't do?"

Her cheeks pinkened. "Lots of things. I don't know how to fly a plane or create the hottest toy of the year. I heard on the radio that your company has one of the most sought-after toys for Christmas. Your miniature robo ball is wildly popular."

A smile pulled at the corners of his mouth. "It's sold out. We're checking to see if we can get more produced and shipped before Christmas, but it's going to be close."

"Then it sounds like you're a hit."

"Not me. The toy." He glanced down at the phone in his hand as it buzzed. "I should be going."

He leaned forward to kiss her goodbye. It seemed so natural. So right. And then he spied the wide-eyed surprise on her beautiful face.

He pulled back. "I'll, uh, see you at home."

"See you there."

And with that he walked away. He couldn't believe he'd almost kissed her. It hadn't been anything he'd planned. It just seemed like the right thing to do in the moment.

Things were changing between them. Quickly. But he wasn't ready to examine the implications.

He was a man on a mission. He pulled out his phone to contact his assistant. He wanted meetings set up for the rest of the day with various departments. There was no time to waste.

He knew it was far too late to implement the homemade biscuits and treats in the grand opening, but he wanted to be able to announce it at the grand opening. It was the perfect time to grow a swell of interest. And it would be the perfect thing to help Pepper now and in the future. But would she agree to sell him her recipes?

CHAPTER THIRTEEN

HOW HAD THINGS gotten so comfortable?

Three days later, Pepper moved around Simon's enormous kitchen in her bare feet as though she'd lived there for years. The gleaming white tiles were cold to the touch, but with the dual ovens going, the air was quite warm and the coolness of the floor felt good to her.

She glanced up to find Simon in the doorway, staring at her with a smile on his face.

"What?" she asked, feeling self-conscious. "Do I have batter on my face?"

He shook his head. "No. You just look cute in your jeans and apron. Maybe instead of being called the polka-dotted baker, we should call you the barefoot baker."

She glanced down at her holly berry dazzle nail polish. She wiggled her toes, letting the recessed lights catch the sparkles and make her toes twinkle.

She lifted her head and smiled at him. "You like them?"

"Actually, I do. And with that red ribbon around your ponytail, you look like you're ready for a Christmas party."

"Hardly. I'm a mess."

He stepped up to her. He stopped just inches from her. "If this is you looking a mess, I like it."

He was flirting with her? Heat swirled in her chest and rushed to her face. She wasn't sure what to say. When he was looking at her like she was a cherry that he was eating up with his eyes, her thoughts scattered and her ability to make quick comebacks utterly and completely left her.

But knowing that she had to get this order done in the very near future, she said, "You know, instead of standing around talking silliness, you could be helping."

"It's not silliness." His voice lowered as his gaze caressed her face. She could feel the way his gaze moved over her just as surely as if he'd reached out and touched her. "You are beautiful. Don't ever doubt it. Both inside and out."

"Thank you." Now her face felt as though it were pressed against the hot oven. A trickle of perspiration ran down her cleavage. She resisted the urge to fan herself, but if Simon didn't move away soon, she was afraid her entire body would go up in flames.

"No need to thank me. I'm just stating a fact." And still he stared at her with a smile on his face.

He had no idea how much she just wanted to toss aside the bowl of batter and melt into his embrace as her mouth sought out his. But that wasn't part of their arrangement. They'd agreed to this living arrangement just until she completed her Christmas commitments. By then, her apartment over the bakery should be deemed safe to move back into.

Until then, she had so much to do. And then she realized that Simon was home early—earlier than normal on a Monday. "Why are you here?"

His dark brows rose. "Am I not allowed to leave work early without suspicion?"

She shook her head, swishing her ponytail over her shoulder. "Sorry. That's not what I meant."

"It's okay. I was just giving you a hard time." He stepped away from her and suddenly she missed having him so close to her.

"I thought you had some important meetings today."

He rubbed the back of his neck. "I did. But I

rearranged them and got them done earlier than I had originally planned." He glanced around the kitchen. "Looks like I wasn't the only one busy."

She followed his gaze, taking in the sight of bowls, pans, spoons and numerous other kitchen items dirty and in need of cleaning. "Sorry. I just had so much to do today that I couldn't keep up with the cleaning, baking and decorating." She glanced at the timer. She didn't have long until the current batch of cupcakes came out and the new batch went in, if she wanted to get all of this delivered in time for the party. "I'm sorry. But I have to get back to work."

"Don't let me hold you up."

She turned to the kitchen island and continued to fill each cupcake liner three-quarters full. She struggled to keep her attention on the task at hand and not on the way Simon had been looking at her. Things were definitely changing between them. The thought sent a shiver of excitement through her.

In the background, she heard water running. She wondered what Simon was up to. She desperately wanted to turn and check him out, but she denied herself that privilege. She had a deadline and she needed to keep her attention focused on her work.

Yeah. Like that was going to happen.

She tilted the bowl up and moved to the next empty cupcake liner. She reminded herself that just because there was obvious chemistry crackling between them, it didn't mean they should forget what they'd agreed to. Roommates. Nothing more. Because soon she'd be going back to her apartment—if the fire marshal would release the scene so she could start the repairs—and she had to keep her attention on the bakery.

When the tray of cupcake liners was filled and the dribbles wiped clean, it was ready for the oven. Pepper turned and placed the bowl on the counter. It was then that she spotted Simon. He had his sleeves rolled up as he worked in a sink full of soapy water. With the top buttons of his dress shirt undone, he looked totally adorable as he hand-washed a pan for her. What in the world had gotten into him? Whatever it was, she liked it.

Still, she should tell him to stop. This wasn't his responsibility. Part of their agreement was that she would see to the upkeep of the kitchen. But with the soapsuds on his arms, he looked utterly irresistible. Some woman was going to be very lucky when she landed him.

Pepper didn't know where the thought had

come from, but it totally dampened her mood. The thought of him cooking and cleaning in the kitchen with another woman made her stomach sour. She dismissed the thought, shoving it to the far recesses of her mind.

Now more than ever, she needed to get him out of the kitchen. As sweet as he was to help her without her even asking, he was that much of a distraction. And tonight's party was very important. She couldn't mess things up.

The apartment phone rang, which usually meant it was the doorman. Simon dried his hands before answering it. She couldn't make out what he was saying.

Pepper looked up from where she was pouring batter into the cupcake pans. "Are you expecting guests?"

He shook his head. "It's the fire marshal."

Immediately, concern coursed through her. "What do you think he wants?"

"I guess we'll find out."

She still hadn't gotten past the part where the fire captain had mentioned arson and then looked at her like she was guilty. If this was going to be more false accusations, she wasn't going to stand by and take it.

Just then the timer for the other oven went off. She sighed.

Simon glanced over his shoulder at her. "It's okay. You take care of things in here and I'll get the door."

She didn't have any choice but to nod in agreement. The last thing she needed was to ruin a batch of cupcakes, or worse, fill Simon's penthouse with smoke while the fire marshal was there.

Pepper swapped the finished cupcakes for the unbaked ones. She'd just set the timer when she heard Simon call out her name. She slipped the timer in her pocket, as she didn't have time to make another batch should these ones accidentally stay in the oven too long.

She headed for the door, all the while preparing herself for more false accusations. When Pepper approached the foyer, she found the two men having a relaxed conversation. She wasn't sure how to react.

When the fire marshal's gaze caught hers, he said, "Ms. Kane?"

She nodded. He stuck out his hand, giving hers a brief but firm shake.

"I'm Inspector Hayes. I've just completed a total review of the fire at your bakery. I know you and Mr. Ross have been very interested in the results."

Interested? That was an understatement. When you're accused of arson, you want your good name cleared as soon as possible.

A denial of any wrongdoing hovered at the back of her mouth, but deciding that it would just make her look guiltier, she held back. Instead, she said, "What have you found?"

He lifted a black leather binder and flipped it open. His gaze scanned the page. "I noticed that you've recently had the bakery remodeled. Is that correct?"

"Sort of." She wondered if everything she said to him was about to be used against her.

As though Simon was reading her thoughts, he asked, "Is this something she should have an attorney for?"

The fire marshal's head lifted and surprise filled his eyes. "Oh, no. I'm sorry. I should have started with the fact that the fire has been ruled an accident. There was some faulty wiring in the kitchen."

"Oh." It was all Pepper could muster as the relief hit her.

The fire marshal flipped back to the top sheet.

"I just have a few questions that I need answered before I can finalize the report."

He asked Pepper about the remodel, the date of the remodel and a few other questions. And then he said, "And that should be it. I'll make sure the insurance company gets a copy."

"Am I free to get into the building?" Pepper asked.

"Yes. But I'll caution you to be careful. You're going to want a clean-up crew in there before you try to do anything."

They thanked the fire marshal for stopping by and completing the report so quickly. As the man exited the penthouse, Pepper felt like the end of this chapter of her life was looming in the near future. Because once the apartment was cleaned up, there would be no need for her to stay with Simon. Was it wrong that the thought of going home no longer thrilled her? Had the short time she'd spent with Simon made that much of a difference?

Because the longer she was here—the longer they were together—the more she wondered what might have been. And she just couldn't afford to give her heart to someone else that would leave her. She'd been left behind by everyone she'd loved in her life. She couldn't do it again.

CHAPTER FOURTEEN

AT LAST THE day had come…

A frigid Tuesday morning made even the snowmen dotting the sides of the streets, dressed in colorful scarves and assorted hats, shiver. A fresh layer of snow blanketed all of New York City.

As Pepper stood on the sidewalk outside her bakery, she didn't notice the cold or the flakes landing on her hair and coat. A gust of wind rushed past them. Pepper stood like a statue staring forward at the place she'd once called home—still called home, even in its total state of devastation.

The outside of the bakery was still stained with soot trailing up the front of the white painted bricks. Plywood covered all the windows.

The back of her eyes stung with unshed tears. Her stomach made a nauseous lurch. She struggled to maintain her composure.

She blinked. The nightmare was still there,

playing out in a slow, excruciating sequence. Would the interior be better than she was imagining? Or worse? Her palms grew clammy. She didn't want to see the inside of the bakery—yet she had to see it.

A hand touched her back. "You don't have to do this."

She turned to Simon. "Yes, I do."

Concern flooded his eyes. "I'm here for you."

"I know. Thank you."

She squared her shoulders. She was stronger than this. She'd buried her mother. She'd buried her grandmother. In the grand scheme of things, this was a setback, not the end of the world. So then why did it feel like it?

She forced herself to take one step and then another.

She lifted the caution tape and then stepped beneath it. With shaky hands, she opened the door. Taking a deep, calming breath, she stepped into the darkened room. Even in the shadows, she could make out enough to know that everything she'd worked for—everything she'd loved—was charred and ruined.

She switched on the flashlight app on her phone. The stream of light highlighted one slice of the room at a time. Everything was layered with dark soot. The glass display cases were covered in debris and the fronts were cracked or broken.

This is bad. So very bad.

The light landed on the shelves behind the counter. There was Bugles McBeagle. Her heart ached. She rushed forward, tripping over the debris on the floor.

Simon's hand reached out, catching her arm. He held on until she'd regained her balance. "Be careful. There's a lot of mess on the floor."

She nodded because she didn't trust her voice. Emotions had clogged her throat. She continued moving toward the stuffed animal that she'd owned most of her life. It had so many memories attached to it, from her mother giving it to her to holding it when she'd packed her bags and moved in with her grandmother. It had seen her through all the tumultuous times in her life—including this one.

She knew it was silly to be so attached to an inanimate object, but she couldn't help it. Losing Bugles was like losing an important piece of herself. She reached up to the shelf and wrapped her fingers around the stuffed dog, surprised to find it was still in one piece. She pulled it down. It had soot on it, but other than that there didn't seem to be any other damage. How was that possible when it looked like a war had been waged within these walls?

"Pepper?" Simon's voice drew her out of her thoughts.

For a moment, she'd forgotten he was here with her. He was being so quiet and letting her walk through the bakery at her own pace.

Holding Bugles close, she said, "I... I'm okay."

What else was she supposed to say? That she was utterly devastated? That she felt as though her life had been ripped out from under her? That she didn't know where she would find the strength to start her life over once more?

They moved toward the kitchen. This was where the real devastation had taken place. Things in here were charred. Her beautiful stainless-steel appliances were black now. Her utensils were melted unrecognizable blobs. Her heart cracked a little more.

Simon stepped in front of her. He reached out and gently swiped a tear from her cheek. She didn't even know she'd been crying.

"Pepper, look at me." His soft voice coaxed her.

She didn't want to. Taking her gaze off the

devastation took effort. When she did stare into his eyes, she saw sympathy in his eyes.

His hands gripped her shoulders. "You'll get your bakery back. It'll be better than ever. And I promise to do whatever I can to help."

She shook her head. "It's my problem. Not yours."

"But I want to help. Please let me."

She didn't say a word. Right now, the fight had gone out of her. She just needed a moment to wrap her mind around the fact that the bakery of her dreams was gone. Sure, she could build a new one, maybe even a better one, but it would never be the same.

He felt terrible.

Simon had some inkling of an idea what Pepper was feeling. And it wasn't good.

They'd both created their own happiness. His happiness had been in creating toys—toys he'd wanted so much as a kid but couldn't have because his father lost one job after another. Her happiness had been found in the kitchen creating the most amazing treats—treats that he surmised reminded her of the family she'd lost. In that they had a special bond.

But if his company were to be ripped out from

beneath him, he couldn't even imagine the devastation he would feel. He glanced over at Pepper, who was doing her best to maintain her composure. He admired her strength. He wasn't sure he would be able to stand tall in similar circumstances.

Now, as they toured her apartment above the bakery, he could see a glimmer of hope in her eyes. It was much better than the downstairs, as the fire hadn't reached this floor. Still, the heavy odor of smoke clung to everything. When Pepper went to pack some clothes, her nose curled up. Still, she kept grabbing things as though she worried she'd never see any of it again—photos, binders and some kitchen items.

He carried her things out to the car and placed them in the trunk. He'd never seen such a look of utter despair on a person's face. His heart ached for her. If it was within his power to rectify this nightmare, he would in a heartbeat. But this was a project that was going to take time to make right.

Certain Pepper had had more than enough for one day, he coaxed her out of the building. She walked ahead while he secured the building. He turned to find she'd made her way down the walk. He rushed to catch up to her.

When she passed by his car, he didn't say anything. After the lingering scent of smoke, the fresh air was a welcome relief. As they continued walking, he noticed the snow had lightened up. Getting through the city would be slow going but it was still doable.

It wasn't until they were at the end of the next block that Pepper stopped. She turned to him. "Where's the car?"

He pointed over his shoulder.

"Oh. Sorry. I was lost in my thoughts."

"No problem."

"But you have to get to the office."

"The office can wait."

She arched a fine brow at him as though she was trying to figure out if he was being serious. "We better go."

When he didn't move, she made her way past him. Tracking through the inch of new snow, she led the way back to the car. He followed her, knowing he needed to say something encouraging. Yet he struggled to find the right words.

At the car, he opened her door. She paused in front of him. She lifted her wounded gaze to meet his. "Thank you for being so understanding."

"I wish I could make this all better for you."

"I know." Her voice cracked with emotion.

He stepped toward her and pulled her into his embrace. He didn't have any other words to offer her. He only had his shoulder to offer. Her whole body leaned into him. They fitted together as though they'd been made for each other. Her gentle breath fanned over his neck and warmed his blood.

He turned his head just slightly and inhaled her lavender scent. He would never smell lavender again without thinking of her. He pressed a kiss to her head.

When she pulled back, his gaze moved to her rosy lips. He wanted to kiss her again. He wanted to wash away her worries and sweep her up in a moment of passion.

He hesitated. She'd been through so much, inspecting the damaged bakery. He wasn't sure she would welcome his advance. And he wouldn't do anything to make this day more stressful for her. Kissing her would have to wait for another time.

With great reluctance, he stepped back. She climbed in the car and then he closed the door. He crossed in front of the car and then climbed in. Once the engine was started and the heat turned up, he paused.

He hadn't been planning to have this conversation with Pepper just yet, but after seeing her turmoil today, maybe now was best. It wasn't like him to rush into anything. He liked to take a slow and cautious approach. But what he was about to propose he knew was the right thing—for both of them.

"Simon, what's wrong? Is it the snow?" Concern rang out in her voice.

He leaned back in his seat. His gaze caught hers. "It's not the weather. I want to talk to you."

"About what?"

"There is something that I've given a lot of thought. I wasn't planning to bring it up just yet, but there's an urgency to it. I have a proposal for you—"

"No, Simon. We already talked about this. A marriage for the baby's sake would never work—"

"Whoa. Slow down. My apologies for giving you the wrong impression. My proposal isn't one of marriage. It's a business proposal."

Her perfectly plucked brows drew together. "Business proposal? But I don't have a business—at least, not right now."

He drew in a deep breath, figuring out the best way to explain his vision. "Do you remember when I visited you at the shelter?" When she nodded, he continued. "That's when I got the beginning of an idea. Remember those snacks you baked for the animals?" When she nodded, he continued. "Well, I'd like to buy the rights to the recipes."

"What?" Her mouth gaped.

"I promise to make it a lucrative deal with you receiving a percent of future sales." Normally, he wasn't a generous businessman, but this wasn't just any business deal. He was dealing with the mother of his child—the woman who'd given Christmas back to him.

"But why?"

He smiled. "I guess I skipped right over that part." He cleared his throat. "I've mentioned the Pet Playground store chain that we're opening." When she nodded once again, he continued. "I knew there was something missing from it—something that would take it from being just another pet store to something exceptional. I'd been racking my brain for that special element and then you presented it to me. A gourmet bakery in each store. It will cater to the pet owner that wants something special for the four-legged friend." When Pepper didn't immediately respond, he started to worry. "What do you think?"

"I think it's a wonderful idea."

"Would you consider being my partner? You know, with the recipes, making sure the bakeries are set up properly and approving the staff?"

She didn't say anything for a moment. "I've never been involved in something like this. It sounds enormous."

"It would be, but it won't work without you."

"I like the idea. Really, I do. But I have my hands full getting the bakery back up and running."

"I thought you might say that so…" He reached in his coat pocket and pulled out a business card. "I took some liberties and contacted my best contractor. This is his card." He handed it over to her. "He's waiting for your call. His men have been on standby, waiting for the building to be given the green light."

She accepted the card and read it. "You mean these men are being paid to stand around, doing nothing, while waiting for my call?"

He nodded. "I hope you're not upset, but I wanted to help."

She didn't say anything and he worried that perhaps he'd gone too far. He knew waiting times for contractors could be quite long—especially in the city. He'd only wanted to help.

She pulled out her phone.

"What are you doing?" he asked.

"I'm calling your contractor—who is now my contractor. I'm giving them the go-ahead to clear the debris. And those binders you were so nice to carry to the car have my original notes and plans for the bakery. I'd like to make it look as close to the original plan as possible."

"I like that idea. The bakery was perfect." And there was one more thing he needed to know. "And the idea for the gourmet pet bakery?"

"I love it. But I have one condition."

He'd thought that he'd proposed a very generous offer, but it wouldn't hurt to hear what she had in mind. "Let's hear it."

"I'd like a portion of sales to be donated to animal shelters."

He smiled. "That's a fabulous idea. It's a deal."

They shook on it.

He had a feeling that both of their futures were going to benefit greatly from this union. Now Pepper would be in his personal life as they raised their child, and in his business world too. The thought of her always being around brought him a happiness he'd never known before.

CHAPTER FIFTEEN

"WE HAVE A PROBLEM."

The next afternoon, Pepper gripped the phone tighter. "What sort of problem?"

Stephanie sighed. "I don't think we should discuss it on the phone. Can you come to the shelter right away?"

"Actually, I'm on my way to meet with my insurance agent—"

"I wouldn't ask if it wasn't urgent." There was a desperate tone to Stephanie's voice that Pepper had never heard before.

She'd just been at the shelter yesterday afternoon. Everything had been all right then. What could have gone so wrong so fast?

"You're worrying me. Please tell me there's nothing wrong with Daisy."

Silence was the only response.

Pepper's heart lurched. Daisy was so sweet and had so much love to give if she would just learn how to trust people again.

And then a worrisome thought came to her. What if someone had seen Daisy, even though she wasn't ready for adoption yet? What if they'd bonded with Daisy and wanted to take her home?

Pepper's heart sank. She knew that was the danger of volunteering at the animal shelter. Each and every stray that came through that door just wanted to be loved. And Pepper loved them all. If she could, she'd take them all home. But there was something about Daisy that truly tugged at her heartstrings.

Stephanie knew how she and Daisy were starting to bond. Of course, Pepper would drop everything to be there for the beagle pup. Besides, she doubted that a face-to-face meeting with her insurance agent was going to produce any faster results than her daily phone conversations.

"I'll be right there."

After a quick, apologetic phone call to her agent, Pepper rushed to the shelter, not sure what sort of problem she would find. She prayed Daisy was all right.

She stepped inside the shelter and didn't notice anything amiss. She moved toward Stephanie's office. "What's going on?"

"It's Daisy. She has to go."

"Go? Go where?"

"Daisy can't stay here any longer." She looked as though she had the weight of the world upon her shoulders. "Greta has demanded the dog be gone."

Pepper immediately frowned. Nothing good could follow the mention of Greta. In fact, she was quite certain that woman lacked a heart. If ever there was a Grinch, it was Greta. And sadly, the woman was in charge of the shelter. Pepper never did understand how that had happened.

Stephanie stood, moved around her desk and stepped to the doorway. She glanced up and down the hall before closing the door ever so gently, as though not to make a sound.

Pepper's worries increased. She'd never seen her friend act so oddly. She couldn't imagine what was wrong, but if Greta was involved, she knew it had to be bad. That woman was a menace.

Stephanie spoke in whispered tones. "Greta is claiming that Daisy bit her."

"What?" Pepper couldn't believe what she was hearing. "Sweet Daisy wouldn't hurt a fly. Sure, she growls, but that's just because she's scared. She doesn't mean it."

"I know that. And you know that. But Greta doesn't like her."

"She doesn't like her because I like Daisy."

"I don't know. I just know Greta is claiming the dog is dangerous."

"Daisy is a puppy." With every passing moment, Pepper was growing more and more defensive about the puppy. "And she's not dangerous."

"The thing is, Greta says Daisy has to go. Today."

"But this is a shelter. This is where homeless dogs are supposed to go." This couldn't be happening. She was finally making headway with Daisy. The puppy was learning to trust her. "She isn't ready to be adopted."

"That's the thing. With Greta claiming she was bit—which I checked and I couldn't even see a scratch on her—I can't adopt out Daisy."

"What…what will happen to her?"

"I told Greta I would make sure Daisy is gone before tomorrow. Otherwise, she says she's taking matters into her own hands. And you know that won't be good."

Chills ran down Pepper's arms. "I don't know why that woman even works here, much less is in charge."

"You know and I know that it's for the money. And the fact she pulled strings to get the job."

"It's not fair to the people who work here and

certainly not the animals. She doesn't even like animals."

Stephanie held up her hands helplessly. "At the moment we're stuck with her."

"And Daisy?"

"That's what I'm hoping you can help me with."

"Me? How?" She would do anything to save Daisy.

"I need you to take her home." Before Pepper could say anything, Stephanie held up a finger to pause Pepper's rebuttal. "Listen, you and I both know that's what you were working toward. Maybe you weren't willing to admit it to yourself just yet, but Daisy belongs with you."

She was willing to do anything for Daisy... but take her home. "I don't have a home to take her to. Remember? The fire."

Stephanie's gaze pleaded with her. "But you said you were staying in Simon's great big apartment."

"It's a penthouse. And the man who's letting me stay there doesn't like dogs. Or cats. Or anything that can make a mess, makes noise or needs taking care of." She thought she remembered all his reasons not to have a pet. How exactly was he going to deal with a baby?

Stephanie's mouth gaped. "And he let you stay with him?"

Pepper shrugged. "I clean up after myself."

Stephanie shook her head. "Surely there has to be a place you can keep Daisy until your apartment is ready."

Pepper thought of everyone she knew, including her second-in-charge at the bakery, but her daughter had asthma and was allergic to most pets. And there wasn't anyone else she would feel right about imposing on.

And then her gaze landed on Stephanie. "What about you?"

"You know I would if I could. But I've already taken in three dogs. One more and my landlord has threatened to kick me to the curb. Besides, I don't think Daisy will go with anyone but you."

"But Simon is going to throw a fit."

"Better him than Greta."

"True. But still… He might toss me to the curb."

Stephanie sent her a knowing smile. "You forget I saw him when he came to the shelter. I saw how he hung on your every word. I don't think you have a thing to worry about."

Was she serious? Pepper was never quite sure where she stood with Simon. Some days she thought he liked her just fine and other days she felt like she was nothing but in the way—another problem for him to deal with.

And now with Daisy, well, she was certain he wasn't going to take it well at all. But she couldn't let Greta do away with the puppy. Chills rushed over her skin. That woman was just pure evil. The shelter would be so much better off without her. If only there was a way to get rid of Grinchy Greta.

"Pepper, you have to decide now."

"Fine. I'll take her." She forcefully blocked out what this would mean to her relationship with Simon.

She probably should ask him before taking the puppy home, but this way she was saving him from having to say no and from her having to ignore his wishes. It still didn't leave her in a great position, but perhaps she could move back into her own apartment, even though it wasn't finished.

And so Stephanie set her up with everything she'd need to care for Daisy, including a crate. One of the volunteers offered to give her a lift back to the penthouse. Pepper could only hope it was early enough that Simon wouldn't be home yet.

She took the private elevator from the underground garage to the top floor. Pepper caught herself holding her breath as she entered the penthouse and looked around. Today was the housekeeper's day off, so that definitely helped things. To her great relief, Simon wasn't home.

She placed Daisy on the marble floor of the foyer. Immediately, the puppy had an accident. Oh, boy, they were not getting off to a good start.

"Don't worry," she said. "I'll get you in the bedroom and then I'll come back to clean it up."

Pepper led Daisy down the hallway to her bedroom. Along the way, Daisy took the time to investigate her surroundings. Her nose was going a mile a minute as she inspected everything in the wide hallway.

Daisy was like a new dog now that she was out of the shelter—much more relaxed. "I'm so sorry you've had a rough start in life. But don't worry, you'll be safe and hopefully happy from now on."

Pepper wasn't sure what the future held for the two of them. She was starting to wonder if there were any motels in the area that she could afford and that took pets.

She knelt down in front of Daisy. The puppy

sat down and looked at her with those big brown eyes that instantly melted her heart.

Pepper moved slowly so as not to scare Daisy with any sudden movements. In the great big bag that Stephanie had packed, she found Daisy's stuffed blue bear. At the sight of it, Daisy's tail started to wag.

Pepper held it out to her, but Daisy didn't move. "It's okay. You can have it."

Still Daisy didn't move. Pepper placed the bear on the floor in front of Daisy. Immediately, Daisy gripped the bear with her mouth. The bear was almost the same size as Daisy. But that didn't keep Daisy from dragging the stuffed animal over to the fuzzy white rug next to Pepper's bed. There the dog lay down and put her head on the stuffed animal.

Pepper watched Daisy for a moment to make sure everything would be all right. Daisy's eyes started to grow heavy. She'd had a really big day. Pepper cringed at the thought of Grinchy Greta yelling at the puppy. That woman. Pepper's back teeth ground together as she held back a string of heated words. Daisy didn't need to hear Pepper vent. The pup needed some peace and quiet to get used to her temporary lodgings.

When Simon found out about Daisy, Pepper wasn't so sure they'd have a roof over their—

"Pepper!"

Oh, no. Simon is home.

And by the tone of his voice, he was not happy.

Daisy's head immediately lifted. And in a second or two both she and the teddy bear scooted under the bed. Poor baby.

"Pepper!"

"Daisy, it's okay. His bark is worse than his bite. I'll be back." She wasn't so sure about letting the puppy lose in a room with expensive decorations, but Simon obviously wasn't in the mood to wait.

She rushed out of her bedroom and down the hallway. She skidded to a halt when she noticed the angry look on his face.

"Are you all right?" he asked.

She nodded.

"No accidents or anything that I should be aware of?"

Heat rushed to her face. Did he know about Daisy already? Had someone spotted them coming into the building and told him?

She shook her head. All the while she tried to figure out how to break the news gently to him. Was there any way to tell a man who didn't have pets, who didn't want pets, that there was now one living in his house?

"Mind explaining this?"

She followed the gaze to the floor—and his stocking feet. "You took your shoes off?"

He shook his head and pointed. His new-looking black dress shoe was sitting in the dog pee. Ugh! She'd hoped to clean that up before he got home. Daisy's homecoming was getting off to an even worse start than Pepper had imagined possible.

"I can explain."

Simon pressed his hands to his trim waist. "I'm listening."

"I was going to clean up the mess."

"Why is there a mess in my otherwise immaculate foyer?"

By the stormy look on his face, nothing she said was going to make this better. She might as well just go pack her stuff—not that she had much to pack.

This couldn't be happening.

His neat, formerly clean, quiet life was being upended.

Simon moved to the living room in his stocking feet. All the while, Pepper followed him, telling him about the drama of her day. And this person named Daisy.

He held up his hands. "Who is Daisy?"

"Didn't you hear me?"

The truth was, he'd been wondering how one five-foot-five woman could take his otherwise routine life and spin it on its head. Not only was she living with him, she was having his baby and now Daisy was staying with them.

He cleared his throat. "I have a lot on my mind."

Pepper looked uncertain of what to say.

Arff! Arff! Ooh-whoo!

"What in the world?" His gaze narrowed in on Pepper, whose face filled with color. "Do you have a dog in here?"

Arff! Arff! Ooh-whoo!

"I'll explain in a second."

"You'll explain now." He frowned at her. "You know I don't want pets."

"But if you just give me a chance to explain, you'll see that there really wasn't any other alternative."

Arff!

"I'll be back." Pepper turned and rushed out of the room.

She couldn't just walk away. They weren't finished with this discussion. He followed her down the hallway to her room.

Pepper opened her bedroom door and out rushed a puppy.

"Daisy," Pepper called.

But the dog didn't listen. Simon should have known it wouldn't even be trained. The puppy rushed right up to him and then stopped to sniff his pants and then his feet. He recognized the puppy from the shelter.

He wanted to be angry. He'd told her point-blank when she'd tried to talk him into adopting a dog that it wasn't for him. He was better off alone. But this dog was still a puppy. He knelt down to pet it. And it was sort of cute.

"Be careful," Pepper said.

He glanced up at her. "You brought home a vicious puppy?"

"Well, no. But…but she doesn't really know you. And she's not sure where she is."

He turned his attention back to the puppy. He let her sniff his hand and then he ran his hand over her smooth coat. She certainly didn't seem vicious.

Simon scooped up the puppy and straightened. He arched a brow at his flustered houseguest.

"I think you should come with me and explain why this puppy is running around the house."

"Just a second." Pepper ducked into her room and returned with a blue teddy bear.

He wasn't quite sure about the necessity of the stuffed animal, but maybe it was a new baby toy that she'd picked up.

Simon turned with Daisy in his arms. He continued to pet the dog and she remained contentedly in his arms. In the living room, once he sat down, Daisy wiggled to get off his lap. He set her down.

Pepper joined the puppy on the floor and waved the teddy bear in front of Daisy. The puppy took hold of the teddy bear and moved beneath the coffee table.

"The stuffed animal is for the dog?" he asked.

Pepper finally smiled. "Yes. Daisy loves her stuffed animal. She always sleeps with it."

"Interesting." He continued to watch the dog as it left the teddy bear on the rug as it began to explore the room.

"I'll get her," Pepper said.

"Leave her. She isn't hurting anything." And then under his breath he said, "At least not yet." He cleared his throat. "Tell me more about this puppy."

And then Pepper went back to the beginning and told him everything, about the puppy, from its tragic past to the Greta woman accusing Daisy of being a vicious dog.

"I take it you don't like this Greta?"

"Like her? I can't stand her. Neither can anyone else at the shelter. My friend Stephanie could run the shelter if given a chance. Instead she's Greta's assistant, aka the person who does all of the grunt work but gets none of the credit."

He recalled how the pushy woman had hit him up for a donation. His gut told him the animals wouldn't benefit from the money. His investigators still hadn't come up with any concrete evidence against her. Perhaps it was time for him to contact Greta about a five-figure donation.

The more he thought about it, the more he liked the idea. All he had to do was provide the bait and he was certain Greta's greed would do the rest.

He made a mental note of this. He may not want a pet, but that didn't mean he didn't care. And whatever upset Pepper upset him—

Hold it.

When had that happened?

"Simon, what's wrong?" Pepper looked at him

with concern in her eyes. "If it's Daisy, I'll go stay at the apartment."

"You can't."

Her fine brows drew together. "How do you know?"

"Because I stopped by at lunchtime. The apartment still isn't ready for anyone to live there. But don't worry, I put more men on the job. They'll be working round the clock."

"But how? I don't even have the insurance straightened out."

He shrugged. "It doesn't matter."

"It does matter. How am I ever going to pay you back?"

"Pepper, stop worrying. If I didn't want to do it, I wouldn't have. Everything is fine."

She opened her mouth and then closed it. For a moment, they both watched as Daisy nosed her way around the room. And then Pepper turned back to him. "I'll get my stuff. Daisy and I will find a motel."

"No." He couldn't believe he was saying this. "You and Daisy will stay here."

"But you don't want her here."

"Are you trying to talk me out of it?"

She shook her head. "I'll try to keep her out of sight."

Just then Daisy meandered over to him and sat on his foot. "Don't make promises you can't keep."

Pepper rushed over, scooped up the puppy and grabbed the teddy bear. She started toward her room. She paused and turned back to him. "Thank you. I just couldn't let anything bad happen to Daisy. She's already gone through so much as a puppy."

And then both Pepper and the puppy were gone. He sat there for a few minutes, thinking Pepper would return so they could finish their talk. But as the seconds turned to minutes, he realized the puppy was going to change things between him and Pepper—similar to the way the baby would change everything.

Maybe he should rethink things. Maybe Daisy could be a trial run for them—learning to share responsibilities. The more he thought of it, the more he realized he needed all the practice he could get—even if it was with a puppy.

CHAPTER SIXTEEN

IT WAS GETTING LATE.

And he still wasn't home.

Thursday evening, Pepper ate her dinner on the couch with Daisy next to her. The pup had become her shadow. If Pepper ever had any thoughts of rehoming Daisy, they'd been quickly forgotten.

Still, this was the first time Simon had said he would be home for dinner and then was a no-show. She never thought this arrangement would work out. In fact, she'd been downright certain it was a huge mistake, from the press hounding them, to the unexpected news of the baby—her hand pressed to her slight baby bump—to the fact she couldn't let herself fall for him.

Simon didn't do commitments. He'd told her that.

He also normally didn't work nine-to-five. So then why until now did he make such an effort for them to share their breakfasts and most dinners—even sometimes slipping home for lunch?

He was going out of his way to make her comfortable. Again, she came back to the question: *Why?* She told herself it was because he was just being a good host. Nothing more. But then why did it feel like more? Why did it feel like they'd become some sort of an insta-family? And if that was the case, where did they go from here?

Daisy lay in the corner of the kitchen, where she could keep an eye on Pepper. Talk about your loyal companion. Pepper smiled. "You're a good girl."

Daisy lifted her head and wagged her tail, understanding what Pepper had said.

And then because she couldn't resist such cuteness, Pepper grabbed a dog biscuit from the plastic bag on the counter and gave it to Daisy, who readily accepted it.

With the dirty dishes rinsed and loaded in the dishwasher, the countertops wiped down and nothing left to do for the day, she glanced at the clock. It was well past six. Where was he?

Don't worry. It's none of your business. He's only your host. Nothing more. Except the father of your baby.

Did that make a difference? Enough for her

to butt into his life and make sure he was okay? Their situation was so complicated. She wasn't sure what was right. And what was inappropriate.

She glanced at her purse on the bar stool at the giant island. Sticking out of the top was the mail she'd picked up on her way back from the animal shelter. A padded manila envelope snagged her attention. She was pretty certain what was inside—a new-to-her DVD.

She didn't care if some people called her old-fashioned. She loved black-and-white movies. She collected them. Though some were available for streaming, a vast number were not. She had a huge collection of VHS tapes she'd inherited from her mother, and slowly over time she was replacing them with DVDs.

She pulled out the package. Maybe she should sit down and get lost in a movie. After all, she was caught up with everything she had to prep for tomorrow.

Her gaze strayed to the clock on the wall. It really was late for Simon. Worry settled over her, dampening her mood. Where could he be?

Silly question. She assured herself he probably got wrapped up in a project at work and forgot the time. She knew how that could be. When she was developing a new recipe, she could be at it for hours until she got just the right match of ingredients.

Maybe she should call him, just to make sure that was the case. She moved to get her phone from the counter next to the fridge. She picked it up and pulled up Simon's number.

Her finger hovered over the call button. Should she? Or would it be overstepping? What would Simon think—

She heard the sound of the front door opening. She set her phone aside and rushed out of the kitchen, with Daisy right behind her. There stood Simon in the foyer. His black wool overcoat glistened with quickly melting snow.

He slipped off his coat and hung it up to dry. He glanced up. "Sorry I'm late. It's getting nasty out there."

"You're late?" She tried to act like it was no big deal—like she hadn't been worried about him. "I hadn't noticed."

He arched a disbelieving brow at her. "Are you trying to tell me that you haven't eaten yet?"

Heat rushed to her cheeks. She'd been busted. "I tried to wait. Honest."

He smiled. "So, you did notice my absence?"

Heat licked at her face as she shrugged. "I

guess I got used to our routine. I started to worry when you didn't show up." Now what in the world had she gone and said that for? "I mean, I know you have a lot of work to do and sometimes you have to stay at the office late."

"Actually, I didn't work late."

"You didn't?"

He shook his head. "I stopped by the bakery. I wanted to see the progress."

"The bakery?" Was he getting anxious for her to move out?

He nodded. "I was curious how things were going. But no one was there."

"I was there earlier. They're waiting on the city inspector. He should be there tomorrow morning. I intend to be there when he arrives."

Simon's gaze met hers. "Are you sure you're up for everything you have going on?"

Her chin jutted out just slightly, as she didn't like the thought of being judged differently because she was carrying a little human inside her. "I'm managing just fine—at least until the baby arrives."

"Okay then. I will leave it to you to handle. But if you need anything—anything at all—tell me." He bent down to greet Daisy.

"I will." There was something more she'd been meaning to tell him. "Thank you."

"You don't need to thank me—"

"I do. You helped me through one of the most difficult times in my life." She took a deep breath. This admission wasn't easy for her. "My life has a lot of difficult twists and turns. I felt as though I'd finally got my footing and then the fire happened." She blinked back the sudden rush of tears. "But you helped me through it. I don't know what I'd have done without you."

"You didn't need me. You are amazingly strong—stronger than you give yourself credit." His eyes reflected his sincerity. "But I'm glad you think I was able to help you in some manner."

"They say the bakery will be up and running by the end of January. But I don't know. There's so much damage."

"If it takes more men, I'll make sure you have them."

He really was in a rush to get rid of her. She lowered her gaze to Daisy, who was sitting next to her. Pepper had definitely overstayed her welcome. But he was too much of a gentleman to tell her that he was tired of having her here in his space. Now that the situation with the insurance had been cleared up, there were funds for temporary housing.

"Hey," he said, "stop looking so worried. I was going to say that my selfish reason is because I miss your coffee and cherry turnovers."

"Really?" When he nodded, she took her first easy breath. "I was worried that you were tired of having me around."

He frowned at her. "It never crossed my mind. Besides, when you leave, I'll probably go back to takeout instead of the home-cooked healthy options you make."

She couldn't help but notice how he said "when," not "if." Her heart sank.

"Are you up for a little more business this evening?" he asked.

She shoved aside her worries about the future. "Sure. What do you need?"

"I have the contract for your recipes for the gourmet bakeries. Can we go over them?"

She nodded.

And so for the next hour or so, she read the contract. They discussed various points. And he took notes of her idea for the bakeries. The fact that he took her and her ideas seriously touched her.

Ting. Ting. Ting.

Pepper turned to the darkened windows. "Do you hear that?"

Simon nodded. "Sounds like an ice storm. Don't worry. It'll blow over quickly."

She somehow doubted that a winter storm would blow over quickly. For some reason, winter storms seemed to linger, unlike summer storms that would roll in and out in a very short amount of time. Or maybe it was the short days in the winter that made the bad weather feel like it lingered.

The lights flickered.

"That's definitely not a good sign." Her gaze moved to him.

"I'm sure it's nothing big."

Pepper's gaze again moved to the window. Deciding that Simon was right and there was no point worrying about it, she asked, "Have you eaten yet?"

He shook his head. "I didn't have a chance."

"Well then, you're in luck. I made spaghetti and homemade meatballs. I had a craving."

He arched a dark brow. "Isn't it early for those?"

She shrugged. "I've been known to have cravings without being pregnant. I'm guessing it's going to be a full seven months of continuous cravings."

"That should be interesting. Any desire for pickles and ice cream?"

Her nose scrunched up. "That sounds utterly revolting."

"I agree. I was just checking to see what I was in for."

She walked to the kitchen, pulled the plate of spaghetti from the fridge and placed it in the microwave. Her gaze moved to the window above the kitchen sink. The ice was continuing to hit the window. A shiver raced over her skin. She'd never liked winter storms. She didn't like the feeling of being cut off from everyone else; that's why she'd always lived in the city.

Simon stepped up to her. "What's got you rattled?"

"It's just the weather."

"It's more than the weather. Talk to me."

She shook her head. "It's nothing."

"It's something and I'd like to know, if you'll tell me."

Pepper gave herself a firm mental shake, chasing away the bad memory. Retrieving the warmed plate from the microwave, she turned to Simon. "Where would you like to eat?"

He shrugged. "The living room is fine."

Pepper handed him the plate and then retrieved

a fork and napkin. She led the way. She settled on the couch and then lifted Daisy to her lap.

He glanced at the movie on the coffee table. "Is that what you were planning to watch?"

Simon, as she was quickly learning, wasn't a television-type person. He'd rather bury himself in reports or read a book, which was fine by her. To each his own. But she didn't want to bore him with her passion.

"It's nothing I can't watch another time," she said, settling back on the couch.

He set aside his untouched dinner. He picked up the DVD case and read the front before turning it over to read the back. "Interesting."

"Really?" She was totally caught off guard. "I didn't think you were into movies."

"I take it you enjoy them."

"I love them. I have an entire collection of old movies." And then she was reminded of the fire. "That is, unless they were destroyed."

"How many movies do you have in your collection?"

"Over three hundred."

"That's a lot of movies."

"I guess I inherited the interest from my mother. She was quite eclectic, which is obvious by the name she chose for me because I was born on Christmas Eve."

"I don't think Pepper is all that rare."

"No. My full name." When he looked at her as though he didn't get what she was trying to tell him, she said, "Pepper Mint Kane."

His mouth opened and his lips formed an O. "I didn't know. That is a bit unique."

"No. It's horrible. Do you have any idea what the kids did to me in school?"

"I'm guessing you wanted to change your name."

She nodded. "My name. My school. My life."

"So why didn't you when you got older?"

She shrugged. "What was the point? The worst of it was over and by then I'd lost my mother." Not wanting to go further down this path, she said, "Anyway, I've been working on replacing my mother's collection of VHS tapes with DVDs. I'm guessing not too far in the future I'll be replacing the DVDs with newer technology."

"Are they all older movies?"

She nodded. "This Cary Grant movie…" she gestured to *An Affair to Remember*, which was in Simon's hand "…is one of my all-time favorites."

"Isn't it a bit depressing?"

She shrugged. "I guess it depends on how you look at it."

"And how do you look at it?"

"That true love can conquer anything—sometimes it just takes a little bit of effort. But never give up."

Simon looked at her strangely.

"What?" She felt a bit self-conscious under his direct stare. "Simon, stop looking at me like that."

"It's just in all the time I've known you, I never knew that you were a romantic."

"I'm not a romantic." Was she? She'd never really thought about it. "I just like romantic movies."

"Then put it on and let's watch it."

"Seriously?"

"Of course."

He didn't have to tell her twice. She started the DVD, turned off the lights and settled on the couch, leaving a respectable distance between her and Simon. Daisy decided the empty space was just perfect for her and her teddy. And so by the glow of the fireplace, they watched the movie. Even when Simon finished his dinner, he remained.

And then without warning, the power went out midway through the movie.

They both waited quietly for the power to flicker back on, but as the seconds ticked away, the darkness persisted.

Simon moved toward the window and looked out. "Seems we're not alone in the dark. Hopefully, it won't be off for long, but at least the fireplace still works." He turned to her. "Maybe we'll be camping in the living room tonight."

Pepper wrapped her arms about her. She didn't say anything as she was drawn back in time to another place—another time.

"I'll get us some blankets." Using the flashlight app on his phone, he headed toward the bedrooms.

In the short amount of time he was gone, Pepper told herself to quit acting like this power outage was such a big deal. The fireplace would keep them warm and the power company would surely have the lights on in no time. This wasn't the past.

"Pepper?"

She didn't say anything. She didn't trust her voice. And she didn't want to make a fool of herself. After all, it was a power outage. No big deal. But during a winter storm, the chances of the power returning soon weren't very good.

He moved to her side, opposite the dog. "Pepper, talk to me."

"I don't like power outages."

"I don't think anyone likes them, but they seem to bother you more than most. So tell me about your childhood. It might help pass the time."

Her mind flew to all the embarrassing, hurtful things in her past.

Her palms grew damp as her stomach churned. She just couldn't imagine peeling back the layers and exposing herself to him in that way. And that made her a bad person for not wanting to share. She knew it.

But what Simon didn't know was how hard it had been for her to let him this close to her. She knew that people could show the world one face and then in a blink pull off their smiley mask and reveal another, more sinister face.

She turned to Simon. She studied his very handsome face with its strong lines and mesmerizing eyes. Did he wear a mask? Her heart told her that he didn't, but her mind told her to beware.

Perhaps she'd start with why she didn't like bad winter storms. It wasn't like it was a big secret or anything. "It was a long time ago, when I was just a little girl. I remember it being a particularly cold and snowy winter. There was just me and my mom. I never knew my father."

Simon reached across the couch cushion, placing his hand over hers. She found warmth and comfort in his touch. "That's why it's so important to you that I have a close relationship with our baby?"

Pepper nodded as she gazed down at their hands. "My mother was working two or three jobs to make ends meet, but then she lost a job and we had to go without electricity for a couple of very long days and nights. I'd never been so cold in my life. It had been horrible. We'd huddle around a kerosene heater."

"I'm sorry. That must have been scary for you."

"I'm sure you never had to worry about anything like that."

"Pepper, I didn't grow up rich. For the most part, my mother raised me as a single mom too."

"Really?" When he nodded, she added, "It's just that you fit so well in this lifestyle. It's like you've been doing it all of your life."

He shook his head. "I didn't start to make any real money until I was in college. I liked to tinker with things. I always did. But then I started creating things and getting patents."

"That must have been so exciting."

"It was, but I had to overcome a lot of obstacles to make it that far."

"What was your childhood like?"

He shrugged. "Sometimes it was awesome. It was like having the perfect family. But the illusion only lasted for moments at a time. The other times, it was a nightmare."

Pepper felt guilty for thinking her childhood was so difficult. They might have been short on money, but the house had been full of love. It sounded like Simon's childhood home was anything but loving.

"Okay. So I told you my story. Now it's my turn to ask you a serious question. Why don't you like Christmas?"

The doors to the past once again creaked open.

Maybe if he opened up to Pepper, she would understand why they didn't belong together as a couple. She would know how damaged he was and want to keep a respectable distance instead of looking at him with need and desire that was so hard for him to resist.

If they were going to be a family, he didn't

want there to be any secrets. He needed Pepper to make sure he didn't turn into his father—that could never happen.

Simon cleared his throat. "My father was an angry man and when he drank, he hurt everyone in his path." He paused as though to gather his thoughts. "There were some days when he was fine, almost human. But most days…most days you just wanted to stay out of his way. And holidays, well, those were the worst."

The memories came rushing back to him in sharp, jagged pieces. Each of them slicing into his scarred heart. And then the long-buried anger and resentment came roaring forth.

"I was nine that Christmas. I was long past the Santa stuff, but my mother shooed me to bed early anyway. She told me I couldn't see my presents until the morning. My father was out, so the house was quiet—almost peaceful— except the silence was more ominous than relaxing."

His mind rewound time until he was back there. He remembered vividly his nine-year-old self, so sure he was no longer a child.

"I'd fallen asleep, anxious for Christmas. I never got a lot of presents, but my mother worked hard to make sure I got one special toy and some clothes. I don't know how long I'd been asleep when I was wakened by the sound of my parents fighting. It wasn't uncommon, but this time it was so much worse than the others. Things were crashing against the wall. My mother was screaming. And my father was out for blood."

Simon glanced over at Pepper. She was quiet and her eyes showed sympathy. But she didn't stop him. So he kept going, leaving the grisly details out for both of their sakes.

"With my mother bleeding, I tried to stop my father—reason with my father. But he'd had too much to drink and he was too full of rage." His voice cracked with emotion. He couldn't stop here or he'd never get the rest out. "I was too small to stand up to a man who did manual labor all day long, but I gave it my all—giving my mother a chance to defend herself. And when I just couldn't anymore, I dragged myself to the phone and called for help."

Pepper leaned into him, wrapping her arms about him. "I'm so sorry."

"The police arrested him. My mother and I spent the rest of the night at the hospital getting stitches, and our broken bones treated."

He could feel the dampness of Pepper's tears seeping into his dress shirt. He wrapped an arm around her shoulders. She fitted there against him as though they'd been made for each other.

"When we got home on Christmas, we saw how the tree had been destroyed, the ornaments shattered. The whole place looked like a bomb had blown up in it. I told my mother I never ever wanted to celebrate Christmas again. She didn't argue. I knew she didn't want to relive that night."

"I'm sorry. I had no idea when I brought home the tree what you'd been through."

"Actually, it was good for me. You helped me see that I was stronger than those memories. So thank you for helping me see Christmas Present instead of Christmas Past."

"Your father... Do you ever see him?"

"No." That was another story of its own. "My mother refused to testify against him. But I refused to let him hurt us again. I got up on the stand and I sent my father to jail."

Pepper pulled back. "You are the strongest person I've ever known."

"My mother didn't think so. I don't think she ever forgave me for sending him to jail. And then when he died during a riot, it was my fault he died. My mother and I had a very strained relationship after all of that."

She might have been there physically for the milestone moments of his life, but she hadn't been there emotionally. They didn't speak to each other about the important things in life. He never wanted to be like that with his child.

But with his parental role models, he felt doomed. Except there was Pepper. She was filled with sunshine and rainbows. With her to help him, maybe he could be the type of father he'd always wanted—patient, understanding and loving.

"Your mother seemed happy about the baby." Pepper's voice drew him from his thoughts.

He nodded. "She did, which surprised me."

"Maybe it's a chance for you two to reconnect."

"I wouldn't get your hopes up. I've been taking care of her financially and I thought it would make a difference, but there's still this chasm between us."

"Have you tried talking to her about it?"

He shook his head. "The past is best left alone."

"What about just opening up to her about what's going on in your life now? Maybe she isn't sure what to say to you. Maybe if you took the first step…"

He'd never tried because he didn't think his

mother cared. But could Pepper be right? Was his mother waiting for him to make the first move?

"I don't know," he said. "I think she still blames me for his death."

"The woman I saw, who got so excited about her future grandchild, didn't look at you with anything but love in her eyes."

"Really?"

"Really. Give her a chance. You might be surprised."

He turned so he could look directly at Pepper. "And what about you? Do you regret getting involved with me now that you know just how damaged I am?"

She reached out and cupped his cheek, her fingertips brushing over his face. "I think you are strong, kind and resilient. You are not damaged. You are the perfect man to be a father to our baby…"

"But what if I turn out like my father?"

"You won't."

"How can you be so sure?"

"Because of the way you've cared for your mother, even though you think she blames you. And for the way you've cared for me, even before you knew about the baby. You have a good

and honest heart. This baby will be all the better for having you in his or her life."

Her words were a balm upon his scars.

He leaned forward and pressed his lips to hers.
How had he been so lucky to have Pepper in his
life? She didn't see him as a rich man with connections; she saw him as he really was, warts
and all. And still she was here in his arms.

Her mouth moved beneath his with a hunger
of her own. Why exactly had he been holding
her at arm's length? The reason totally eluded
him now.

And so with the heavy snow falling outside
and the puppy cuddled with her teddy on the
couch, Simon and Pepper moved to the nest of
blankets and pillows in front of the fire. It was
there that he held her in his arms and made tender love to her, showing her just how much she
meant to him.

CHAPTER SEVENTEEN

THIS WAS A bad idea.

A very bad idea.

And yet Simon let Pepper talk him into inviting his mother to the grand opening of the first Ross Pet Playground. He'd tried to tell her that his dysfunctional relationship with his mother was better left in private, but Pepper had looked at him with that pleading look in her eyes.

What was it about her that got to him? If it had been anyone else, he would have shut them down immediately. But Pepper, she was so optimistic, so caring. Except for the woman she called Grinchy Greta.

His people were uncovering every shady thing in her past. They were also tracking the generous donation he'd made to the shelter. It sounded like the Grinch would be dealt with in time for Christmas. He knew keeping the animals safe from that woman would be the best Christmas gift for Pepper.

Simon waited inside the new store as invited guests lined up on the sidewalk just on the other side of the giant red ribbon. A hired car pulled to a stop. His mother stepped out of the back seat of the black sedan with tinted windows.

She looked particularly pleased, especially when the press recognized her. They took her photo, which she posed for, smiling brilliantly.

Simon inwardly sighed. His mother was no shrinking violet. Once she'd got out from under his father's thumb, she'd shown a surprising amount of spunk. Over the years, she'd made a point of putting herself out there, trying new experiences and meeting new people.

Simon glanced at his watch. Only two more minutes until the ribbon cutting. Even the news crews had arrived. But there was no sign of the one person who he really wanted to be here. Pepper.

She was the one who'd helped him take this pet shop to a new level with its gourmet bakery. With her recipes, it was going to be a huge success. He'd really wanted her to stand up here and cut the ribbon with him, but she'd refused.

But later, they'd share a private celebration with a glass of sparkling grape juice and a kiss beneath the mistletoe. He couldn't wait. He had an early birthday surprise for Pepper.

Ninety seconds to go.

"Are you ready?" his assistant, Elaine, asked. He nodded.

Another car pulled up. It was a business associate. Simon restrained a frustrated sigh. Behind that car was another. Would it be Pepper?

No.

He shoved aside his thoughts of Pepper, who would be here soon, just like she'd said she'd be. Instead, he needed to focus on this moment. Today was about... What was it about? It was more than a new store opening—much more. And it was no longer about conquering yet another challenge. His thoughts came full circle.

Today was more about Pepper. As she was the one who had given him the drive to make this a success—for more than himself. And Pepper would see that, if she would just show up.

"It's time," his assistant said.

He forced a smile to his lips as he kept checking to see if she'd arrived. He was so disappointed that she was going to miss this, because he had a surprise for her. One he was certain she would approve of.

But with the cameras rolling, he couldn't stall.

The show, as they said must go on. He stepped outside. A round of applause rolled over the crowd.

"Thank you all for coming." All the while, his gaze scanned the crowd, searching for Pepper. "It seems like forever since we did something special like this for Ross Toys. And thanks to all of you, it's going to be a huge success."

Again, there was applause.

"But this moment is even more special for me because this accomplishment isn't just for me." Simon paused. He'd thought he saw Pepper. He scanned the faces again. Yes, there was she was, toward the back.

Simon placed his hand over the microphone in order to speak to Elaine, who was standing off to the side. "Pepper arrived. She's in the back. Please escort her here."

Elaine didn't say a word but instead nodded and set off to take care of the task.

Simon turned back to the crowd. "Sorry about that. A special guest has just arrived. This person has helped me take Ross Pet Playground from just another pet store to something extra special. I have a surprise announcement that hasn't been released to the public."

A hush fell over the crowd as they waited to hear the news.

"Within each and every Ross Pet Playground there's going to be a gourmet bakery." An excited murmur moved through the crowd. "We will be starting out with dog and cat treats that are not only tasty and cute, but also baked right in the store with top-of-the-line ingredients."

Pepper appeared off to the side of the stage with Daisy in her arms. He gestured for her to join him. She hesitated and shook her head. He gestured again.

"And you have this wonderful baker to thank for the tasty treats." When Pepper stepped forward, he said, "I would like to introduce the Polka Dotted Baker, Pepper Kane."

Another round of applause. Questions were shouted from the press, but Simon ignored them. He wasn't answering any questions until the ribbon cutting was complete. And he still had a surprise for Pepper.

"Pepper has a bakery right here in Manhattan." And then he gave the address. "It is going to reopen in the New Year. I hope you'll stop by and give her your support. Just wait until you try her coffee and pastries. They are out of this world." He glanced over at Pepper, who was now blushing. She looked so adorable.

His assistant handed him a giant pair of scissors. When Pepper started to move away, he reached out to her. "Stay. You're really going to want to hear this next part." He turned back to the microphone. "Before I cut the ribbon, I have one more thing to say. With every purchase that's made at Ross Pet Playgrounds, a portion of the profits will be donated to Daisy's Friends. And if you're wondering who Daisy is—" he moved next to Pepper and gestured to the puppy "—this is Daisy. She's a rescue from a local animal shelter. She left behind lots of cuddly friends who need our help. Funds are limited and Ross Pet Playgrounds want to help by supporting local animal shelters."

The loudest applause of all filled the air.

He gestured for his assistant to come forward. "Can Elaine hold Daisy for just a moment?"

Pepper's brows drew together. "Simon, what are you doing?"

"You'll see." He helped transfer Daisy from Pepper's protective arms to his assistant's, who appeared to instantly fall in love with Daisy. He couldn't blame her. That little dog had a way of worming into the most resistant heart.

He spoke into the microphone again. "Pepper, you've been so instrumental in making this opening a success that I'd like you to cut the ribbon with me. What do you say?"

Her cheeks were rosy as she nodded her head. He gripped one side of the scissor handle and she gripped the other. Together they snipped the ribbon.

And then they moved to the side as the doors swept open and all the guests were ushered inside the store, with its shelves filled with dog and cat toys and Christmas stockings stuffed with pet toys. The shop was decorated with Christmas decorations. In the center was an area for dog training, and along with the bakery expansion there was going to be an adoption center.

"You did a really great job," Pepper said.

Elaine moved up to them and handed the docile Daisy back to Pepper. "I agree, boss. You really outdid yourself."

"But it wasn't me." He was uncomfortable with taking the praise when it was Pepper and Daisy that had inspired the additions to the store.

Elaine turned to Pepper. "I don't know how you did it, but I definitely like the change."

His assistant walked away and Pepper wore a smile.

He was confused. "What did she mean?"

Pepper looked amused. "I think she was referring to you."

"Me? I haven't changed." Had he?

"That was marvelous, darling." His mother stepped forward and gave him a feathery kiss near his cheek. "I must say that I was surprised by the invitation."

"You can thank Pepper. It was her idea. She thought you might enjoy it."

"And I did." Her gaze met his. "Thank you both for including me."

For the first time in forever, he truly believed his mother. She wasn't saying this to impress anyone. Maybe Pepper was right that his mother wanted a chance to mend their relationship.

Pepper elbowed him. He cleared his throat. "I'm glad you could make it on short notice."

"I'll always make time for my family." His mother turned to Pepper. "I'll be seeing you again soon, at the wedding."

"Wedding?" Pepper sent him a distressed look. She was just as appalled at the thought of marriage as he was, which made him all the more certain that what he had planned for that evening was for the best.

"Mother—"

Before he could say more, a reporter made a beeline for them.

"Gotta go, darling." His mother blew him a kiss and then conveniently slipped out to the waiting car and rode away.

He was jealous of his mother. He wanted to slip away from this crowd with Pepper, but he couldn't do that. This was his brainchild and now he had to see that it was a success. And so he put on his best smile and did his best to dodge any personal questions, while attempting to keep the interview focused on the new store.

By the time he finished with the one reporter, there was another lined up. With the temperatures dipping, they moved inside. Simon looked around for Pepper but didn't see her anywhere. He wondered where she'd gone off to. They had things to discuss.

What had just happened?

Pepper entered the penthouse with Daisy in her arms. "Did you hear that, Daisy? You have a charity named after you! That's pretty cool, right?"

Arff!

Pepper smiled. She loved how Daisy tried to have a conversation with her.

"This means other puppies and kitties that are still looking for their *'fur-ever'* homes will have funds for food, blankets and stuffed animals."

Daisy appeared to be done with the chat, squirming in Pepper's arms, wanting to be put down. She released the leash from Daisy's collar and then placed the puppy on the floor. Daisy took off toward the bedroom as though on a mission.

Pepper headed for the kitchen. Her thoughts were all about Simon and how he hadn't acted any different since they'd made love the other night. She thought it would have changed things between them. It'd changed everything for her. She couldn't hide from the truth any longer.

I love Simon.

The breath hitched in her throat as she acknowledged this truth. If it wasn't for the baby opening up her heart again to love, she didn't know if she'd ever have had the courage to admit her feelings for Simon to herself or anyone else.

And she wanted him to love her too. But as more time passed and he acted like they were nothing more than roommates, she worried that he didn't feel the same way. Or maybe she was just letting her nerves get to her.

She moved around the kitchen, placing the

sponge cake layers on the island to frost with mascarpone frosting. She wasn't sure when Simon would make it home, but when he did, she'd planned a small celebration. She just hoped it wouldn't be too small.

She whipped the mascarpone cheese and then added the powdered sugar a little at a time. This was one of her favorite frostings, as it was so light and delicate. It was sweet without being overpowering. It enhanced the cake without taking over.

Daisy, dragging her teddy bear, entered the kitchen. Placing the teddy bear next to Pepper's feet, she lay down. In just a few moments, Daisy's eyes drifted closed. It'd been a big day for all of them.

As Pepper added the frosting to the top of each of the four layers, she thought about how things had changed between her and Simon. He'd come to accept Daisy, in fact, she'd caught them having a conversation the other morning when Simon thought she was still in bed.

He got up early and took Daisy for her morning walk. He even fed her breakfast so Pepper could sleep in. For a man who didn't like dogs, he was wrapped around Daisy's tail.

Was this the beginning of the family that she'd

always wanted? Her heart swelled with hope. After losing her family one by one, she was finally ready to build a new family. Her hand pressed to her slowly growing midsection.

With the cake completed, she positioned it on the kitchen island. And then she retrieved the card she'd picked up. It was a Christmas card, but she'd written him a note on the inside. And then to make the scene complete, she added two champagne flutes and an ice bucket with some sparkling grape juice.

She moved to the living room. Pepper turned on the tree lights and that was all. She loved the soft glow that filled the room. It'd grown dark even earlier than normal.

She moved to the tall window that gave an amazing view of downtown. The overcast sky led her to believe that there was more snow on the way. As if in acknowledgment, a lone snowflake fluttered past the window. She hoped Simon made it home before it got bad out.

She'd just curled up on the couch and turned on the remainder of *An Affair to Remember* when the front door opened.

"Simon, in here," she called out.

He walked in and joined her on the couch.

He glanced at the large screen television. "You didn't get enough of this the other night?"

"Well, it is one of my favorite movies." She arched a brow. "And we didn't get to see the end. Remember?"

"Hmm… I might remember getting distracted." His eyes sparkled with merriment. He was having fun with her.

With the way he was looking at her, with her own desire reflected in his eyes, her face filled with so much heat that she thought her hair would spontaneously catch fire. She remembered every single last delicious detail of what had happened the other night. The thing she didn't know was where it left them. They'd been so busy and so distracted that they hadn't had time to talk—until now.

As she turned off the television, she had the distinct feeling she wouldn't see the end of it tonight either. Though she couldn't complain. This distraction was definitely so much better than the movie.

Still, she was nervous. They had to talk about the future—their future. And though she had a really good feeling about where they were headed, saying the words would make it real.

Her insides shivered with nerves. Not a bad kind of nervous. It was an excited kind of nervous.

She hadn't told him yet, but she loved him. It hadn't happened suddenly, but rather she figured it must have happened slowly over time. Somewhere along the way, as they'd shared their morning coffee and discussed current events, or she'd regaled him with a story about what happened at the bakery the day before, she'd fallen in love with Simon.

Those mornings had seemed so innocent—so laid-back—that she hadn't realized what was happening until now. She was madly, crazily in love with Simon. And now she was having his baby.

And soon they would be one big happy family. Her heart swelled with love. Her happiness overflowed into a big smile that lifted her lips and puffed up her cheeks. They were going to be so—

"I think we should live together," he said.

"What?" She swallowed hard. Was it possible her dreams were coming true? It was time she made her own confession. Her heart hammered so loudly in her chest that it echoed in her ears. It'd be so easy to back out—to keep her feelings to herself.

After all, everyone she'd loved had vanished from her life. What if the same thing happened to Simon?

But she had the baby now. And she loved it dearly. She had faith that the baby would always be a part of her life, now and in the future. If she could believe that, then she could open her heart to Simon. She could believe they'd have a future.

"Simon." She waited until his gaze met hers. "I love you."

He took a step back as though in shock. Was her admission that much of a surprise? Was she the only one who felt that way?

She couldn't drop the subject. When he didn't say anything, she said, "Simon, do you love me?"

"I... I'm sorry. This was a mistake. I didn't mean to get your hopes up that—that we would be more than we are."

Her heart sank all the way down to her bare feet with her pink shimmery nail polish. His invitation to move in wasn't about love. It was about convenience—Simon's convenience.

She thought lots of things, like falling for him was the biggest mistake of her life. She was thinking it was time to pack her bags and get back to reality. Staying here would only allow her to wonder what if, and that was dangerous.

She turned away.

"Pepper?"

"Leave me alone."

With Daisy right behind her, Pepper moved toward the hallway that led to her bedroom as fast as her legs would carry her. Her knees felt like jelly as she moved. She just needed to keep it together until she reached her room and was able to close the door. It was just down at the end of the hall.

"Pepper."

Unshed tears stung the backs of her eyes. She blinked repeatedly, refusing to give in to them. It wasn't much further now.

And then she was there. She slipped inside and closed the door. The weight of reality pushed down on her. She sank down on the edge of the bed. She knew what needed to be done—she needed to pack.

It was time to go, to get her life back on track. The apartment wasn't finished, but it was close enough. The things that were left to do could be completed with her living there. She didn't have any other choice. As it was, she'd stayed at the penthouse too long.

Once she was back in her own home around her own things, she would feel better. Right?

What choice did she have? She couldn't stay here and take the crumbs of affection that Simon was willing to toss her way. And in the end, he would leave too—just like the other people she'd loved so dearly.

Sheer determination was the only thing that drove her body from the edge of the bed to the closet, where she had some shopping bags and her clothes. She made sure to only take the ones that she'd paid for. She didn't do charity and she didn't want to feel any more obligated to Simon than she already did.

Knock. Knock.

"Pepper, can we talk some more?"

She glanced down at the bed, where her clothes were scattered, awaiting their turn to be folded and placed in the shopping bags. "Now isn't a good time."

"Pepper, this is important."

She knew she was delaying the inevitable. The best thing to do was to get this over as quickly as possible. As her grandmother used to say, it was like ripping off the bandage—quick was the best.

Pepper moved to the door on wooden legs.

Dread filled her. She didn't know how Simon was going to react to the news. But it isn't like he should mind all that much. She was just beating him to the punch.

She opened the door and stood there. "I don't think you need to say anything else. The fact is—"

"You're leaving?" He gazed over her shoulder to the bed.

She nodded. "Yes."

A distinct frown marred his handsome face. "And what about the baby?"

"I won't keep you from him or her. I'm sure we can work out a reasonable schedule."

She returned to the bed and continued placing her belongings in the shopping bag. And then she realized what he was waiting to hear. Her thoughts were a chaotic mess or she would have thought of it sooner.

She placed a pair of jeans in the bag and then turned to Simon. "Thank you for everything. You've gone above and beyond for me. I will pay you back. It might take some time, but I will do it."

"And that's it?"

"Yes."

With a grunt, he turned and strode away.

That was the last she saw of him. When she went to leave that evening, he was not in the kitchen nor was he in the living room. She had no idea if he was even in the penthouse. She dropped her keys next to the door. With Daisy in one arm and her meager belongings in the other, she walked out.

Her heart ached for the love that was not reciprocated. How could she have been so foolish? They might have had their special moments in the mornings over coffee and a cherry turnover, but that didn't translate into a life together.

Still, they did have this little one. Her hand cradled her tiny baby bump.

"Don't worry little one. We'll work this out. Somehow."

She hoped.

CHAPTER EIGHTEEN

HE'D CALLED OFF work Monday.

And Tuesday.

Simon found himself utterly alone in his great big penthouse. It was Christmas Eve. And the office was slated to work a half day followed by a catered lunch and the distribution of Christmas bonuses. Handing out the much-anticipated envelopes was a job he took on every year—but not this one.

Today was Pepper's birthday. He wondered if she had any special plans. He had presents for her—kitchen items he'd heard her mention, some brightly colored nail polish because he knew she liked painting her nails, and a diamond necklace because it was beautiful just like her. But with her gone, he didn't know what to do with the packages.

Simon moved from room to room. He'd never felt more alone in his life. He even missed Daisy running around, practically tripping him because she was so excited to be taken outside in the morning.

As he ambled into the kitchen to get some coffee, he paused at the kitchen counter, lacking its usual clutter of recipes, Pepper's phone and the dog leash. He rubbed his hand over the heavy stubble along his jaw. The kitchen was back to its spiffy cleanliness. It felt strange and foreign somehow. It also lacked the homey, delicious scents of Pepper's baking. He missed seeing her move barefoot through the kitchen with a touch of flour on her face and clothes.

Most of all, he missed her smile. It wasn't just any smile. It was a smile that could light up the darkest day. It would warm him from the inside out. It filled him with happiness and the feeling that if he believed enough, everything would work out.

He backed away from the counter without his coffee. He'd lost his interest in it. As he walked out of the kitchen, his thoughts centered on his last conversation with Pepper. Where exactly had it all gone so wrong?

They'd been getting along so well. Laughing, talking, sharing. For the first time in his life, he'd started leaving the office at a reasonable hour. Not because he felt required to do it, but rather because he wanted to go home. He wanted to find out what Pepper had done that day. He wanted to share his day with her. Was that the way happy, committed couples felt?

He moved into the living room. Without Pepper in his life, he felt aimless. He was going through the motions, not caring about anything but figuring out how he had lost the most important woman in his life—a woman who'd brought the joy of Christmas back to him.

He bent over and turned on the tree lights. Memories of the evening they'd decorated it flashed through his mind. Things shouldn't have ended like this.

The doorbell rang. His heart launched into his throat. Was this it? Was this his second chance? Had Pepper changed her mind?

He nearly tripped over his own feet trying to get to the door quickly. He swung it open, expecting to find Pepper, but instead his mother stood there. Her smile quickly morphed into a look of concern.

"I stopped by because I found the cutest toy for the baby." All the while, his mother continued to take in his disheveled appearance. "Is Pepper around?"

He turned and walked away. "She's not here."

The door shut with a soft thud. He hoped that meant his mother had decided to go away and leave him alone with his misery. But then he heard the distinct click-click of her heels on the marble floor.

"Simon?"

He sat on a chair in the living room. He leaned forward, resting his elbows on his knees while he stared at the floor. He couldn't meet his mother's gaze.

"Simon, what is going on? You're worrying me."

"Nothing is going on."

"I know that we aren't close. A fact I would like to change. But even I know you should be at the office. Instead, you are here wearing…are those your clothes from yesterday?"

He glanced at his wrinkled pants and his partially unbuttoned shirt. He hadn't gone to bed last night, so he hadn't seen the point in changing. Actually, his attire was the very last thing on his mind.

"If you don't like my appearance, you can leave." He knew he was being unduly grouchy, but he wasn't up for his mother's penchant for putting on a good show.

She moved to the couch and sat down. "That isn't what I meant. I... I'm worried about you."

"Don't be. I've been getting along by myself all of this time. I'll be fine." Even he didn't believe his proclamation.

"You aren't fine. Anyone can see that." Her voice cracked. "And I blame myself."

He lifted his head, surprised to find unshed tears shimmering in his mother's perfectly made up eyes. "This has nothing to do with you."

"Actually, I think it has everything to do with me."

"You?" He shook his head. "Why would my relationship with Pepper have anything to do with you? She barely even knows you."

"Because I wasn't a good mother to you."

His gaze met hers. He was supposed to argue with her, but words failed him. Instead, he quietly waited to hear what she had to say.

"You were the sweetest little boy." She smiled as she moved her gaze toward the window. "You were so full of love, but your father—"

"Stop." His self-defensive nature reared itself. "We're not going to talk about him. I know that you've always blamed me for his death."

"What?" His mother's face took on a pained look. "No. I never blamed you."

"Sure you did. You barely spoke to me after he was arrested and I testified against him. We've never been the same since."

"And that's because I was ashamed of myself. How could I not be when my nine-year-old son was stronger and braver than me?"

He studied her face, a face which appeared to have aged in just a matter of minutes. His mother suddenly looked so much older.

She licked her lips and clasped her hands in her lap. "I should have been there for you. I… I should have protected you. Instead, you protected me." Her voice cracked with emotion. "You made sure that horrible man paid for his sins."

Was this for real? All these years he'd kept his distance from his mother because he thought she hated him, blamed him, had been a huge misunderstanding. He continued to study her face, searching for the truth.

"You don't blame me?"

"No. Never." Her eyes pleaded with him. "I've blamed myself. I grew deeply depressed for many years. It is only in recent years that I've gotten treatment."

And he would have known all of this, if only they'd talked to each other. That's what he was doing with Pepper. Letting her walk away without talking to her.

"I'm sorry," his mother said. "Please forgive me."

He hadn't known how much those words would move him. He took her in his arms as she wept.

When he at last pulled back, he looked into her eyes, so much like his own. "I love you, Mom."

"I love you too." His mother stood. "I should be going. But please don't let things end with Pepper. She's good for you."

"Why do you say that?"

"Because I've seen you with her. You smile when you're around her. And look!" She gestured to the Christmas tree, "I never thought you'd celebrate Christmas again."

"But she's the one who ended things."

"Did she? Or did you give her no other choice?"

"I asked her to stay here with me—to continue this life we'd started."

"But did you tell her you love her?"

His head lowered. He hadn't done that. He'd been so busy worrying about protecting her from him—from him hurting her—that he hadn't allowed himself to say so. He'd held himself back and in the process he'd hurt Pepper.

He knew how to fix this. But first he had to grab a shower. He scratched at the unfamiliar stubble on his chin. In the shower, he'd formulate a plan.

"Thank you, Mom." He kissed her cheek. "I have to hurry. Can you let yourself out?"

"Certainly. Good luck."

He was already rushing down the hallway, working on the most important proposal of his life.

"Happy birthday!"

Stephanie handed Pepper a pink cupcake and a coffee.

"Thank you."

"I know with you being a baker that it's strange to give you a cupcake, but I didn't want you baking your own birthday cake. It's not as good as yours, but I baked it from scratch. And I ate one just to make sure they were edible."

Pepper smiled. "Thank you. It looks delicious."

"I also come bearing news. You're not going to believe this."

Stephanie stood in Pepper's messy apartment with a mix of glee and awe on her face. Pepper, wearing yoga pants and a big T-shirt, moved back to her spot on the new couch. She placed the cupcake on the end table to eat later when her appetite returned.

The last thing she wanted to do at the moment was entertain guests. But Stephanie was too good of a friend to just turn away. No matter how bad Pepper might feel, she wasn't capable of hurting her friend's feelings.

Stephanie joined her on the couch, as it was the only cleaned-off area to sit. The new chairs were stacked with boxes. Everything was in such disarray that it made Pepper's head hurt.

"Won't believe what?"

Stephanie's eyes lit up. "They hauled away Grinchy Greta."

This got Pepper's full attention. "What? Who did?"

"I don't know all of the details. Most of it was all hush-hush. But I was able to hear them tell her that she was under arrest for embezzling. Can you believe it?"

Pepper's mouth gaped open. "Really?"

Stephanie smiled. "And I'm temporarily in charge. I'm not really sure if that's a good thing, considering there will be audits and changes, but at least the animals will be safe from that woman."

"And this means if she was embezzling the donations, there will be more funds for the animals." Pepper's voice lacked the enthusiasm that this occasion deserved.

"How do you think this happened?"

"I'm not sure." Her mind rewound to her conversation with Simon. He'd been asking a lot of questions about the woman. "But I have an idea."

"Did you turn her in?"

"I would have if I'd known. But Simon was asking a lot of questions about Greta."

"Really? Why would he care?"

Pepper shrugged. "He met her when he stopped by the shelter, and I might have mentioned how horrible she is. And then when I brought home Daisy, I think he understood how miserable that woman is and how she shouldn't be allowed around such sweet, adorable animals."

Daisy came scampering into the room as though she'd heard her name called. Pepper leaned over and picked her up. The puppy wiggled around, so full of energy while Pepper could barely move herself from the couch. She missed Simon—missed the life they'd started to create together. Had she made the biggest mistake by walking away? Would he have eventually come to love her?

"Something tells me that we have Simon to thank for ridding us of the Grinch," Stephanie said.

"I think you're right."

"You should call him."

Pepper shook her head. "I don't think he wants to hear from me."

Stephanie's perfectly plucked brows rose high on her forehead. "Trouble in paradise?"

"I… I left."

"As in you and Simon are over?"

Pepper nodded. "It was never going to work out for us. We wanted different things."

"Really? Because you two seemed so perfect together at the shelter and when I saw you on television together for the grand opening of his store."

"I thought so too. But…"

"But what?"

Pepper drew in a deep breath and let it out. "He doesn't love me."

"Oh." Stephanie frowned. "He told you that?"

"No. But when he asked me to stay—"

"He asked you to stay and still you left."

"Didn't you hear me? He doesn't love me. I can't stay with someone who doesn't love me."

"But you love him?"

Pepper nodded. "When I asked him if he felt the same way, he didn't say anything."

"But you're having his baby. And he wanted you to stay. Wouldn't it be worth giving him a second chance?"

"I don't know if he wants one."

"How would you know unless you ask him?"

Stephanie did have a point. Pepper reached for her phone on the end table. She hadn't paid any attention to it since she'd left the penthouse. There were a number of missed calls. None of them were from Simon. Her heart sank.

And then she stumbled over a text message from him:

Can we meet and talk?

Sure. When?

Top of the Empire State Building? Tonight? Seven?

What an odd choice for a meeting spot.

See you there.

CHAPTER NINETEEN

SIMON STOOD ATOP the Empire State Building.

Alone.

He hunched deeper into his coat with the collar turned up to keep out the frigid breeze. Pepper was late. And if she didn't hurry up, he feared he'd soon turn into a snowman. He'd already gotten some strange looks from other couples as he paced back and forth.

The evening was growing colder with each passing moment. Or perhaps it was he that was growing cold after waiting—for forty-five minutes.

To be fair, he'd been early. She was only… nineteen minutes late. She probably wasn't going to come. This was the second time she'd ended things with him.

He should leave.

What had made him think this was a good idea? Just because they'd watched *An Affair to Remember* and he'd wanted to do something romantic for her—to prove just how much he loved her.

And now the first snowflakes had begun to fall from the inky-black sky. How much longer should he wait? How much longer until he accepted that he'd lost the best thing that had ever happened to him?

There was the elevator. He should go get on it. He must look pathetic, standing here all alone, waiting for a woman who wasn't coming. But his feet refused to move. It was as though if he willed it hard enough, long enough, she would come. Which he knew was totally ridiculous. But the doors to the elevator closed and he remained atop the Empire State Building.

If only she'd give him one more chance, he'd show her just how much she meant to him. But he was also a businessman. He knew when to cut his losses. And so with the greatest reluctance, he told himself that he would get on the next elevator.

He moved inside and waited. While he waited, he replayed the lifetime of memories that they'd shared in just a matter of weeks, from the horrible fire to finding out they were going to be parents. And then there was Daisy. He'd never known that he was a dog person until she came along and stole his slippers. He'd gladly go buy another pair of slippers for her to chew on if his family would just come back home.

His head lowered and he stared blindly at the ground. His heart was heavy. And the weight of misery pressed down on his shoulders.

The elevator doors swung open. He didn't move. It took a concentrated effort to move his feet. There was still a part of him that wanted to cling to hope—

"Simon?"

His heart reacted before the rest of him. It leaped with joy. It took his mind a few seconds to catch up. He lifted his head, needing to see that Pepper was in fact standing there before he let himself believe there was hope for them.

His gaze connected with hers and held. Was she really standing there? Surely he hadn't just imagined her, right?

"Simon, are you all right?" She stepped closer. "You look like you've just seen a ghost."

He didn't dare blink or for one moment take his eyes off her. He didn't want her to disappear. If this was a dream then he never wanted it to end.

"You came."

Her brows drew together. "You said it was important."

"It is. But when it got late, I thought—"

"That I wasn't coming. I'm sorry. There was some sort of traffic jam and it held up everyone." She glanced around. "Are we the only ones up here?"

He nodded. "There were other people here, but they've gone now. I was just about to leave."

"Oh." Her gaze lowered. "Listen, I know we have to talk sometime and work out arrangements for the baby—"

"I'm sorry that things ended the way they did. I wanted to call, but I didn't think you'd want to talk to me."

"I needed some time to cool off—to think straight."

"I hope it helped."

"It did."

This being distant and cordial was killing him. All he wanted to do was pull her into his arms, look into her eyes and tell her how much he loved her.

But he worried that if he did, she would pull away. That what little progress they'd made would end. And he couldn't go back to the utter silence on her part. His world was so much darker without the brightness of her smile.

What had he wanted?

Why was he acting so reserved?

And what was up with meeting here at the Empire State Building?

For a moment, Pepper felt as though she'd stepped onto a movie stage and she was playing a part. But the question was what sort of movie was this to be? A romance? Or a tragedy?

Maybe it was selfish of her, but she wanted more from life. If she didn't take the chance—if she didn't put herself out there—she knew she would regret it for the rest of her life. And if it wasn't possible, she knew raising a child alone wouldn't be easy, but she could do it. It was the thought of not having anyone to share the day-to-day struggles and joys with that made her sad.

Living in the penthouse with Simon had given her a glimpse of what it'd be like to share her life with him. And now that she knew what it would be like, it was so hard to accept less.

She couldn't let this drag out. With each passing moment, her heart grew heavier with sadness and loss. "Did you have some papers for me to sign?"

"Papers?" He looked at her with confusion in his eyes.

She nodded. "Isn't that what you called me here for? To sign some custody agreement papers?"

"Um, no." He shifted his weight from one foot to the other. "I wanted to meet you here so we could talk without being interrupted."

What was he leading up to? She had no clue, but there definitely wouldn't be any interruptions up here. At least until the next elevator arrived.

She quietly waited for him to have his say. With each passing second, her heart pounded harder with anticipation.

"Pepper, I'm sorry. I wish… I wish that things hadn't ended like they did. If I could take it back, I would."

She shook her head. "It wasn't all your fault. It was mine too. I wanted things from you that you couldn't give me. I shouldn't have pushed so hard."

"But that's the thing." He stared deep into her eyes. It was as though he could see through all her defenses and straight into her heart that was beating out his name. "I want to give you those things."

"You do?" Please let her have heard him correctly.

He nodded. "I do. But you know about my dysfunctional family and how I had the worst role model for a father ever. I'm afraid that I'll end up like him."

"That could never happen."

His eyes widened. "You really believe that?"

"With all of my heart. You are a good man, whether you believe it or not. Your nature is to protect those you love, not to hurt them."

He paused. "I never thought of it that way." His gaze searched hers. "I love you."

Those three little words knocked the breath from her lungs. She hadn't been expecting them. In fact, she never thought he would ever say them to her.

And then a sneaky voice in the back of her mind wondered if he was just saying what she wanted him to say. Was this his way of getting her and the baby back under his roof?

If so, she couldn't do it. She needed him to love her one hundred percent, for herself, and it not have anything to do with the baby. Because when she gave her heart away, she wanted it to be forever.

She shook her head, refusing to believe he was

saying the words that she'd longed for him to say. "You're just saying that because you think it's what I want to hear."

"I mean them." His gaze pleaded with her. "I love you."

This couldn't be happening. It was too good to be true.

"You just want me to move back so you'll be closer to the baby."

"I love you and I don't want you to do anything you don't want to do. Whether you live at the penthouse or live above the bakery, it won't change how I feel about you. I love you. It has nothing to do with the baby. I love *you*. And I'll keep telling you that I love you until you believe me. Pepper, I love you with all of my heart."

He reached out and swiped a tear from her cheek. She didn't even know she was crying tears of joy. She desperately wanted to believe him. So what was holding her back?

"Do you still love me?" he asked.

She hesitated. She knew putting her heart on the line could be dangerous. But she also knew that without taking a risk, she could be missing the best parts of life.

She nodded.

"Then trust me." He held his hand out to her.

Her gaze moved to his outstretched hand. What was he up to now? Curiosity had her putting her hand in his. He led her to the outlook.

With the gentle snow falling upon the city, it looked like pure magic. She was definitely in the middle of a movie—a movie of her life. Her heart thump-thumped. And dare she believe that it was going to be a romance? With its very own happy ending?

As though reading her mind, Simon got down on one knee. And then he slipped a box from his coat pocket, opened it and held it up to her.

Her mouth gaped. She couldn't believe her eyes. In just a matter of a few moments all her wishes were coming true.

"Pepper, you are the most amazing woman in the world. You taught me how to open my heart again. You've shown me that love comes in all shapes and sizes. And I would love to spend the rest of my life with you. Will you be my wife?"

He was full of all sorts of surprises. "Simon, are...are you sure?"

"I've never been more certain about anything in my life."

She pressed a hand to her mouth, holding back a squeal of delight. Her wide-eyed gaze moved from him to the diamond solitaire ring nestled in black velvet. "Simon, it's beautiful. I'd be honored to be your wife."

He removed the ring from the box. He took her trembling hand into his own and placed the ring on her finger.

In the background there were cheers and clapping from the onlookers that must have exited the elevator somewhere in the middle of the proposal. And there were flashes from cameras. And this time, Pepper didn't care. She didn't care if the whole world knew she loved Simon Ross.

Inside, her heart wasn't just thumping, it was pounding. Her palms were damp. And all she could think about was what that ring on her hand meant—they were going to get their happily-ever-after.

"Kiss! Kiss! Kiss!"

The familiar chant filled the air. How could they have forgotten the best part of this—the kiss? Simon straightened and swept her into his arms.

"I love you. Never ever doubt it," he said.

"I will always love you too." Her voice was soft as it floated through the air. "Merry Christmas."

"Happy birthday."

He remembered! "Thank you. This is the best birthday ever."

He lowered his head and claimed her lips. She knew she'd never tire of his kisses. In fact, she was quite certain she would remember this movie-like moment for the rest of her life. When she was a little old lady, she would tell her great-grandchildren about this moment—this very romantic moment. And she would end the story with *"They lived very, very happily ever after."*

EPILOGUE

Valentine's Day, the Polka Dotted Bakery

HER SECOND MOST favorite holiday had just moved to first on her list.

And it certainly helped that the Polka Dotted Bakery was back in business and busier than ever. Old employees and customers had found that the mass-produced cupcakes weren't better than Pepper's homemade ones. As busy as they were, on Valentine's Day they closed the shop a little early—for a private engagement.

Pepper and Simon were now officially married.

How was this possible?

Pepper stood in her apartment no longer Pepper Mint Kane, but Mrs. Pepper Ross. She loved the sound of it. But she loved her new husband so much more.

She stared down at the diamond band on her finger and smiled. The truth was that she hadn't stopped smiling since they were declared husband and wife. Mrs. Simon Ross, Mrs. Pepper Ross, or just plain old Pepper Ross. The smile on her lips grew.

"And what has you smiling so brightly?"

She glanced up at her very handsome husband. "I was just thinking that you're never going to be able to top this Valentine's. Ever."

His brows rose. "Is that a challenge?"

Oh, no. He had that look in his eyes that said she was about to lose. But somehow, she didn't think it was possible to lose this particular challenge. "Yes. It's a challenge."

An *I got you* smile lifted his lips. "I know next Valentine's will be even better. Want to know how I know this?"

"How's that?"

"There will be three of us next year."

Daisy barked her disagreement and they both laughed.

"Okay. There will be four of us. It doesn't get any better than that."

"Why did I ever doubt you?" Her hand smoothed down over her growing baby bump. At four months along, her pregnancy was finally showing.

"You'll learn to trust me. My family will always be my first priority."

She reached up, running her fingers gently down his cheek. "I already trust you with my heart."

He caught her hand and pressed a kiss to her palm. "How did I ever get so lucky?"

"I guess it's true what they say, you know, about the way to a man's heart is through his stomach." She smiled lovingly into her husband's eyes. To think she would get to do this for the rest of her life. Her heart fluttered with joy. "We should head out, if we're going to make it to the country house by dinner."

"Are you sure that's where you want our honeymoon? I could call up the jet and have it fly us anywhere in the world."

She moved toward the kitchen, stopping in the archway to place her wedding bouquet of red roses on the counter. She worried her bottom lip. Was he going to be upset if they didn't fly away to a warmer climate?

Her heart raced as she worried. This marriage stuff might have a bit of a learning curve.

She turned to him. "But it's going to snow this weekend. And I thought we could get snowed in together, next to a roaring fire."

He stepped closer to her. "The image is quite compelling. Whatever my bride wants, my bride shall get."

Daisy barked in agreement.

"You aren't upset, are you?"

He wrapped his arms around her waist and drew her close. "Not a chance. If we're really lucky, we'll get snowed in for weeks."

"Weeks?"

"You're right. That's not long enough. Maybe the rest of winter. Because I couldn't think of any other place I'd rather be than holding you close as the snow falls. I love you, Mrs. Ross."

"I love you, Mr. Ross."

Okay, so maybe the learning curve wasn't as steep as she'd originally feared. She lifted up on her tiptoes and pressed her lips to his. In fact, learning just might be half the fun.

* * * * *

LET'S TALK
Romance

For exclusive extracts, competitions
and special offers, find us online:

f facebook.com/millsandboon

⊙ @millsandboonuk

🐦 @millsandboon

Or get in touch on 0844 844 1351*

For all the latest titles coming soon,
visit millsandboon.co.uk/nextmonth

Want even more
ROMANCE?

Join our bookclub today!

'Mills & Boon books, the perfect way to escape for an hour or so.'

Miss W. Dyer

'Excellent service, promptly delivered and very good subscription choices.'

Miss A. Pearson

'You get fantastic special offers and the chance to get books before they hit the shops'

Mrs V. Hall

Visit millsandbook.co.uk/Bookclub and save on brand new books.

MILLS & BOON